MISSION: BLACK

A DIVISION EIGHT THRILLER

A.D. STARRLING

COPYRIGHT

Mission:Black (A Division Eight Thriller)
Copyright © AD Starrling 2016-2018. All rights reserved.
Registered with the UK and US Copyright Services.
Fourth paperback edition: 2024

www.ADStarrling.com
shop.adstarrling.com

Edited by Right Ink On The Wall
Cover design by Deranged Doctor Designs

※

The right of AD Starrling to be identified as the author of this work has been asserted in accordance with the Copyright, Designs and Patents Act 1988. All rights reserved. No parts of this book may be reproduced in any form or by any electronic or mechanical means, including information storage and retrieval systems, without the prior written consent of the author, excepting for brief quotes used in reviews. Your respect of the author's rights and hard work is appreciated. Request to publish extracts from this book should be sent to the author at ads@adstarrling.com. This book is a work of fiction. References to real people (living or dead), events, establishments, organizations, or locations are intended only to provide a sense of authenticity, and are used factitiously. All other characters, and all other incidents and dialogue, are drawn from the author's imagination and are not to be construed as real.

DISCOVER AD STARRLING'S SEVENTEEN UNIVERSE AND MORE

Seventeen Series

OTHER SERIES BASED IN THE SEVENTEEN UNIVERSE
Legion
Witch Queen

MILITARY ROMANTIC SUSPENSE
Division Eight

MISCELLANEOUS
Void - A Sci-fi Horror Short Story
The Other Side of the Wall - A Horror Short Story

CHAPTER ONE

JUNE 2014. GULF OF ADEN, ARABIAN SEA.

THE MAN STANDING OUTSIDE THE COMMUNICATIONS room of the cargo ship yawned and stretched out the kinks in his neck. He adjusted the sling of his AK-47 rifle before leaning against the steel compartment door behind him. It wasn't long before his chin started to droop and his breathing grew slow and deep.

Twelve feet away, in an adjacent passageway, Rachel Carter crouched against a bulkhead. She ignored the cold metal at her back and the vibrations traveling through her boots from the engine room several decks below, her gaze focused on the miniature mirror on a stick she held in her left hand. Through it, she could see the snoozing guard outside the communications room.

She stole a glance at her watch before slipping the mirror inside her tactical gear. Adrenaline surged through her veins. She gripped her Sig Pro tightly in both hands, her muscles tensing in anticipation of the upcoming battle. Right on cue, a male voice started a countdown in the wireless receiver in her ear.

'All stations, this is Alpha One. On my mark in three, two, *one!*'

Rachel twisted, dropped to one knee, and squeezed the trigger twice. A distant explosion shook the bowels of the ship at the same time the bullets left the suppressor at the end of her gun and slammed into the guard's chest and head. He jerked and slid down the door, his grip relaxing on his weapon.

Rachel was up and running before the dead man hit the deck. She grabbed the AK-47, slung it around her neck, and dragged the guard's body down the passage. She was back at the communications room in seconds. She rapped the door twice with her knuckles and stood to the side of the doorjamb.

The sound of gunfire rose from the direction of the galley and the main deck. Alarmed shouts followed in the distance.

Rachel rose on the balls of her feet. By now, the men inside the communications room would know the ship was under attack.

The door opened without warning. An automatic rifle burst into life and a spray of bullets ripped through the doorway. The shots slammed harmlessly into the opposite bulkhead.

Rachel yanked the pull ring on a stun grenade and lobbed it through the opening. She turned, dropped on her heels, pressed her hands over her ears, and closed her eyes tightly. The flash from the subsonic deflagration registered as a bright light through her eyelids, the accompanying bang of the grenade throbbing through her bones.

Footsteps sounded on her left just as she rose to her feet. Two men turned the corner of the passage. They stopped, shock registering on their faces at the sight of a tall, blonde woman in the midst of the battlefield. That brief hesitation cost them their lives.

By the time they started to raise their assault rifles, Rachel had cut them down with the AK-47. She strode inside the communications room and stopped a few steps past the doorway.

The chamber was fifteen by twelve feet. A bank of tables crowded the bulkhead to the left. Sitting atop them were the merchant ship's radio and satellite communication hardware, its lifeline to the outside world. Two men lay groaning on the floor ahead of her.

The hairs rose on the back of Rachel's neck.

Satellite infra-red images over the last twenty-four hours had shown three guards permanently stationed inside the ship's communications room and a fourth posted outside.

Instinct had her dropping to the ground. There was movement out of the corner of her eye. The AK-47 slipped from around her neck and clattered across the floor as she hit the deck. She rolled onto her back and saw a blade swoop across the space where she had been a second ago. She narrowed her eyes.

One thing satellite images didn't tell you was the size of your opponents.

At six foot three and over two hundred and fifty pounds, the third guard was a virtual colossus. Though the flash grenade had incapacitated his companions, it seemed to have had little effect on him.

He charged toward her.

Shit, too close!

Rachel flipped onto her feet, swooped at the waist, and brought her right leg up in a roundhouse kick. Her boot made contact with the man's left ribcage. An 'Oof!' left his lips. He slowed a fraction.

She whipped her Kbar knife out in time to block his blade. Her earpiece buzzed to life.

'Alpha Two, this is Alpha One. What's your status, over?'

Busy trying not to get myself killed!

Rachel jumped back to avoid the knife heading toward her heart. Rage darkened her opponent's face as she continued to evade him, her movements nimble in their deadly dance. He roared and attacked with savage, wild swings of his blade.

She smiled. *That's right, big guy, get angry all you want.*

'Alpha Two, this is Alpha One. I repeat, what's your status?'

Had she not been trying to dodge her opponent's attempt to disembowel her, Rachel would have sighed at the undercurrent of tension in her team leader's voice. She glanced to the right. The fight had brought her next to the communications equipment.

Time to finish this.

She stepped up against the closest table just as the large man barreled toward her, jumped in the air, and drove her left knee into his chest. He grunted and toppled backward. She went down with him, her thighs straddling his upper body. They landed hard on the deck.

He brought his arms up, his knife arcing toward her face while his other hand reached for her throat. She blocked his blade and gritted her teeth as his fingers closed around her windpipe. Instinct would have had her trying to free herself from his grip. She ignored it, switched her Kbar to her free hand, leaned into his hold, and slashed her knife across his neck in a clean movement.

The man's eyes widened as arterial blood started pouring from the gash in his flesh. He dropped his blade and clutched helplessly at the scarlet flow with both hands, a gurgle escaping his lips.

He would be dead in minutes.

Rachel heard movement behind her. The two stunned men on the floor were crawling to their feet. They blinked and shook their heads dazedly, assault rifles swinging wildly in their grips. Rachel rolled off the dying man, dropped on her back, and brought her Sig around and up a second before they depressed their triggers. By the time their bullets peppered the air several feet above her head, her shots had found their flesh with deadly accuracy. They went down hard.

Her earpiece buzzed again. 'Alpha Four, this is

Alpha One. Move to Alpha Two's last known location and prepare to—'

'Alpha One, this is Alpha Two. Comms room secured, over,' Rachel snapped into the wireless transmitter pinned to her tactical gear.

There was a brief silence.

'Roger that, Alpha Two. Stand by for further instructions, out.'

The voice was brisk. Rachel suspected she was the only one who heard the trace of relief modulating Alpha One's tone.

Definitely going to have to have words with him.

❄

CHAPTER TWO

Rachel gathered the dead men's weapons and kept them close at hand while she flicked switches and entered commands into the communications systems, re-establishing vital network connections that had been deactivated by the guards. Screens lit up across the board, indicating the vessel was back online.

Thirty-eight hours had passed since the US merchant marine cargo ship *Nostradamus* was intercepted by pirates two hundred nautical miles from the Horn of Africa, in the Gulf of Aden. With over $50 million worth of prime, heavy, electrical machinery bound for the Philippines and twenty-five crew members on board, the vessel was attacked mere hours after it entered the Arabian Sea.

The ransom demand came just as Rachel's team completed a covert mission in Yemen, where they had captured the leader of a terrorist cell with affiliations to the Taliban.

Formed as part of the U.S. Department of Justice's

goal to combat international drug trafficking, the Foreign-deployed Advisory and Support Teams, or FAST, were the DEA's answer to the military's special ops forces.

Officially, FAST teams were tasked with training foreign narcotic law enforcement units, carrying out counter-narcotics missions, and gathering evidence and intelligence to support U.S. and allied drug investigations. Unofficially, FAST were elite tactical units capable of counterterrorism and direct-action missions on foreign soil, similar to their military counterparts.

Two months shy of her thirty-first birthday, Rachel became one of only a handful of female DEA agents to have successfully completed the arduous selection and training program devised by U.S. Special Operations Command for FAST recruits. The operation in Yemen was her twelfth covert assignment since she joined the team in Afghanistan eight months ago.

Although the mission to rescue the hostages aboard the *Nostradamus* normally fell under the remit of Navy SEALs and Marine Special Ops, Rachel's team was called in on the action as the geographically closest tactical unit to the Gulf of Aden.

Everyone knew siege situations were at their most critical twenty-four to forty-eight hours following first contact.

Beyond that, hostage takers got twitchy and hostages got desperate, leading to a perfect storm that often ended in tragedy.

When the DEA got wind that there were possible

links between the pirates holding the *Nostradamus* hostage and a powerful and ultra-secretive drug cartel in East Africa that had so far eluded the U.S. and its allies' efforts at infiltration and intelligence gathering, it gave the FAST team an even stronger justification to be the unit to attempt the rescue.

Rachel suppressed a grimace. *Would have been nice if it wasn't mission number thirteen though.*

Although she tried hard not to fall prey to baseless superstitions, an Irish upbringing and a grandmother who was more catholic than the Pope made this a tricky goal to achieve. Still, the number thirteen was unpopular even with members of the military special ops forces.

The staccato of gunfire started to die down in the distance. Moments later, the words she had been waiting to hear came over the channel.

'Alpha Team, this is Alpha One. We have control of the ship. Helos are on the way. Stand by for further instructions, over.'

'Alpha One, this is Alpha Two. Standing by, out,' said Rachel.

A sigh escaped her lips. She allowed herself to relax slightly, the guns still close at hand.

Though they had been weary after the mission in Yemen, the chance to save lives and gather intelligence on the elusive drug cartel they suspected had been behind many attempted military coups and terrorist attacks across the northern African continent had galvanized the FAST team into action. This was the kind of stuff they lived and breathed for.

It took them less than eighteen hours to assess, plan, and execute the rescue mission in the Gulf of Aden, with the support of a U.S. Navy amphibious assault ship and a destroyer.

Fifteen minutes later, two UH-1N Huey helicopters touched down on the main deck of the *Nostradamus*. The Marine Special Ops team aboard soon assumed control of the ship from the FAST team.

Rachel handed the communications room over to the two soldiers who came to relieve her.

'You guys did good,' said one of the men. He glanced at the bodies on the floor. 'I hear there are no casualties among your team or the hostages.'

She headed for the door, a small smile on her lips. 'Our team leader runs a tight ship.'

'I hear he's got a good XO.'

The soldier's gaze skimmed her figure, admiration evident in his eyes. His companion elbowed him in the ribs.

Rachel's smile turned into a full-blown grin that caused the Marine's breath to catch in his throat.

'That he has,' she said with a humble nod.

And this XO wants to see her commanding officer right now.

She found Benjamin Westfield, aka Alpha One, on the bridge of the ship, where he stood in conversation with the Marine Special Ops team leader. Lights blazed through the windows of the superstructure dominating the cargo ship's upper deck. In the darkness beyond, she made out the assault ship and the destroyer on a fast approach, the waters of the Gulf parting in white, phosphorescent waves beneath their bows.

Thirty feet below the bridge of the *Nostradamus*, the hostages were being led to the safety of the Huey helicopters. The pirates who had survived the attack knelt in a huddle inside a ring of armed FAST agents and Marines on the starboard side of the main deck.

The ringleader of the pirates lay dead on the bridge. Next to him was another man. This one was very much alive and bleeding heavily from a gunshot wound to the abdomen. He was being attended to by Tom "Hannibal" Cook, aka Alpha Five, the FAST team's medic.

'Yeah, yeah, it sucks to be shot,' muttered Hannibal as the injured man groaned beneath his ministering hands. 'Shouldn't have seized this ship then, should you? Asshole.' He looked up when he spotted Rachel. 'Hey. We thought you were toast when you didn't respond earlier.' He glanced to the left and grinned. 'Ben was having kittens.'

Ben concluded his conversation and frowned at Hannibal.

'I was not having kittens,' he said in a hard voice. His gaze found her face. His eyes softened almost imperceptibly.

Rachel clamped down on the hot emotions flooding her chest as she walked up to him, aware of the Marine team leader's curious glance from the other side of the bridge.

Ben's were the most expressive eyes she had ever seen. Normally the color of the sky, they invariably changed with his emotions. They could be as cold and as bright as diamonds when he got angry or turn the color of sapphires when he was happy. But the color she had come to love the most, the one that made her heart melt and her body tremble, was the cobalt-blue of his irises when they made love.

'Sweetheart, you and I need to have a talk when this is over,' she said quietly, her face impassive.

Guilt flashed across Ben's face. She was the only one close enough to see it.

'I was just worried about my XO.' He paused and dropped his voice to a whisper. 'My very sexy XO.'

Rachel shivered when he surreptitiously touched her hand, his fingers leaving a hot trail on her skin. Sensual images of the last time they had slept together danced across her inner vision.

Not that we did much sleeping, she thought, feeling the flames of desire burn through her core once more.

They first met eight months ago, on the day she landed in Afghanistan to take on the role of XO in the DEA's most active FAST team, the previous agent in that role having moved back to the agency's U.S. headquarters. The attraction between them had been instantaneous and as scalding as the heat of the battles they went on to face together. After fighting their feelings for nearly half a year, they finally succumbed to the undeniable pull that existed between them.

More than the great sex, and the sex was THE best she'd ever had, that *either* of them had ever had, Rachel soon realized she had found her soulmate in Ben. They were compatible in almost every way, not just physically, but intellectually and emotionally, with the same life aspirations and ambitions. It was worth the years of shitty, short, unsatisfying relationships she had endured in the little personal time she had had while she worked her way up the career ladder to be at the top of her field in the DEA.

Ben was the man she wanted to spend the rest of her life with. And she was the woman he wanted to grow old with.

She hid a smile when she thought of the engagement ring in the top drawer of her bedside table in her quarters back at their base in Afghanistan. Ben had proposed at the end of a grueling training day exactly one week ago, while they were both still dusty and sweaty from a ten-mile run in the desert. There had been tears of joy, followed by hours of heated lovemaking that almost broke the bed in his room.

Still, a tinge of sorrow had tainted their happy day. Rachel had applied for a transfer to Quantico, where the other FAST teams were stationed at the Marine Corps Base. Their rapidly burgeoning relationship meant they couldn't work together much longer; to continue to do so would violate the DEA and special ops' rules and compromise the safety of their team on the field. It also meant that, bar a few stolen weeks here and there, they would live apart for a good few years until Ben rotated back into one of the U.S. FAST teams or progressed into a more senior role in the DEA, something his father desperately wanted.

'Nearly patched up,' Hannibal muttered from the

other side of the bridge. 'What the—hey, you shouldn't be moving around so much!'

Rachel looked past Ben.

The injured pirate had rolled onto his front and was crawling across the deck toward the bulkhead where the dead ringleader lay. An incomprehensible mumble escaped his lips. His movements grew frantic, fear evident on his face. Hannibal grabbed his shoulder and frowned at the man's garbled speech.

Rachel froze. Ben tensed. They both recognized one of the Somalian words the man had spoken.

Hannibal paled as he looked in the direction the man was pointing. From his position beside the pirate, the DEA agent could see under the table next to the bulkhead.

He turned and shouted, '*BOMB!*'

The last thing Rachel saw was Ben moving in front of her.

The last thing she heard was the explosion.

The last thing she felt was scorching pain as her body drifted helplessly through the air, skin crisping and flesh succumbing to flames and pressure waves from the blast.

Then darkness engulfed her, scattering her hopes and dreams to the winds.

❄

CHAPTER THREE

February 2015. Washington D.C.

Vivian Thorpe leaned against the wall of the rundown boxing gym and watched the woman working the heavy bag on the other side of the room.

She swung her fists and knees relentlessly, her blows landing with an energy that spoke of her rage. Sweat dripped from her face and down her neck, dark patches blotting her sports vest. Tendrils of short, wet, blonde hair clung to her nape.

Though she was a good twenty feet away, Vivian could see the faint marks on her arms. She was aware from the medical reports she had read that there were more beneath the training gear the woman wore. She was also conscious of the reason why she was punching, jabbing, and kicking that bag so hard, putting the whole weight of her scarred body behind her every strike.

Vivian knew all too well about inner demons. After all, she was in love with a man who had had to fight his own for a long time.

She waited another ten minutes before pushing away from the wall and crossing the room.

At this late hour, the gym was practically deserted. Only the manager remained, his shadowy form visible against the flickering lights of a TV behind the window of the tiny office near the changing rooms.

Vivian stopped several feet from the woman and cleared her throat.

Rachel Carter whipped away from the heavy bag and turned to face her, body braced for battle and grey eyes burning with a light that answered the question Vivian had been mulling over the last two weeks.

Hostility was replaced by recognition.

Rachel frowned. 'Hawk?'

Vivian smiled faintly. "Hawk" was the name she had earned while serving in the Marines.

'It's good to see you, Rachel.'

Rachel cocked her head and examined her with a calculating expression that reminded Vivian strongly of Alex Slade, her lover and boss. She was now certain she had made the right choice in seeking this woman out.

The subject of her interest glanced around the empty gym, suspicion darkening her eyes. 'What do you want, Hawk?'

Vivian did not blame her for her wariness.

Eight months after the events that had led to the death of two members of her FAST team and a Marine

Special Ops team leader, Rachel was still not back on active duty.

Had it not been for Benjamin Westfield's quick action, she would also have died that day. As it was, his body protected her from the brunt of the blast. Thrown clear of the bridge of the merchant ship where her team had just successfully rescued a group of hostages, she was cast into the cold waters of the Gulf of Aden some two hundred feet below. The ocean put out the flames scorching her body, minimizing the degree of the burns she sustained. She would have drowned had a Marine not spotted her among the burning debris littering the Arabian Sea.

She was in hospital for eight weeks and returned for further skin grafts over the months that followed. Although her injuries had healed, the DEA remained unconvinced she was ready for the field and was trying to push her into a desk job.

From a physical point of view, she was back on form and at the top of her game. Her psych reports were another matter.

According to the shrinks working her case, Rachel had still not worked through the anger and grief of losing her team mates. To quote one of them, she was "full of rage" and "a potential liability to any team".

Vivian had grimaced when she'd read the reports. She had known Rachel when she was still part of the Marines, where one of her jobs had been to train new FAST recruits in tactical fieldwork in Afghanistan. Rachel was hands down one of the best operatives

Vivian had ever worked with. She knew a desk job was the last thing the DEA agent wanted or needed.

And it would be a damn loss for this country if it were to happen, Vivian thought darkly.

Luckily, she had an alternative path for her. It remained to be seen whether she would choose to accept it.

A heavy sigh brought her back to the moment. Rachel glanced pointedly at her watch.

Though she knew damn well Rachel had nothing to go back to except an empty apartment, Vivian appreciated her unsubtle show of impatience. The woman in front of her was not someone you could push around easily.

'Do you have a moment?' said Vivian. 'I want to talk.'

Half an hour later, Rachel sat back in her seat and stared at Vivian from the other side of a booth. They were in the diner across the road from the gym. Although it was gone one in the morning, they were not the only customers in the restaurant. A truck driver was engaged in small talk with the waitress at the counter. Five tables away and on the opposite side of the aisle, a young man with glasses and a pale complexion surfed the Internet on his laptop.

Rachel had showered and changed into jeans, a T-shirt, and a black bomber jacket. A scar peeked past the neckline of her shirt, where a jagged piece of metal had torn through the flesh above her left collarbone. Her wet hair had dried and curled around her jaw, framing her slim neck and face. Despite the fact that she wore no make-up and bore dark circles under her eyes, she was still very attractive, a fact that was not overlooked by the men in the diner. In comparison, their gazes shied away from Vivian's dark hair and hazel eyes. Her other nickname in the Marines had been "Ice Queen".

Rachel's eyes mirrored the incredulity in her voice. 'You want me to lead a black ops team?'

'Yes,' said Vivian. 'I take it you've heard of Division Eight?'

Rachel raised an eyebrow. 'You mean the rumored black ops section that's not meant to exist?'

Vivian smiled.

Division Eight, also known as "Crazy Eights" and "Black Dogs", was cloaked in secrecy, its existence a rumor among law enforcement organizations and U.S. Armed Forces alike. The brainchild of Alastair Caldwell, the current Director of U.S. National Intelligence, Division Eight was still in its infancy yet had achieved more in its three years of existence than some of the more established military and federal black ops divisions. A retired Admiral, Caldwell served in the Navy for nearly four decades before his appointment to one of the most powerful roles in U.S. government. His actions, though unpopular with some, had seen a fundamental transformation in the way the National Intelligence Program and the Intelligence Community worked to safeguard U.S. interests and security. None could deny that he produced results.

Lying behind Caldwell's ethos was the belief that different branches of the U.S. government could work together in a way that amplified their combined skills and expertise, making them a more effective and deadly fighting force. With that end in mind and the President's blessing, he set about creating Division Eight, an elite tactical unit made up of not only the best operatives and soldiers from intelligence agencies and military special ops around the country, but also the sharpest minds from U.S. science and tech academies.

Although Division Eight answered directly to Caldwell and the President, there were some in Congress who wanted the elusive unit to be subject to more control. Caldwell was fighting back. By hook or by crook, he intended to keep them operational and autonomous. So far, he was winning.

Division Eight's mandate was simple. Their mission was to deal with anyone and anything that challenged the interests and security of the U.S. and its allies, anywhere in the world. Trained to operate in a variety of hostile environments, they were the embodiment of agility and adaptability. They were also subject to plausible deniability if they were ever compromised during a mission in enemy territory.

You did not apply to become a member of the "Crazy Eights". You got asked.

And just as Vivian had been recruited by Alex Slade to be his second in command in the very first Division Eight team, she was now enlisting Rachel to come on board as the leader of EAGLE, the latest team to be formed under the aegis of the commander-in-chief of the United States government.

When she'd spoken to Alex a few weeks ago about approaching Rachel, he had immediately agreed. Like her, he had seen past the DEA agent's physical scars and damning psych reports to her undeniable potential. And just as Alex had once needed Division Eight to overcome his dark past, Rachel Carter needed and deserved a similar opportunity. Division Eight was likely her only remaining chance to show the world what she was truly capable of and serve her country as she so desperately wanted to do. And Vivian had no doubt that the new team needed Rachel just as badly as she needed them.

'What do you know about the Division?' she asked.

Rachel shifted in her seat and crossed her arms over her chest. 'They are the cream of the crop, the very best of military and agency operatives in this country. They operate under the direct command of Alastair Caldwell, the Director of U.S. National Intelligence. They have an unlimited budget and access to the latest weapons, tech, and intelligence available to the U.S. government. They are heavily trained in clandestine operations.' She shrugged. 'They basically deal with the stuff no one else wants to take on.'

Vivian masked her surprise behind an inscrutable stare. 'Seems you know a lot about them already.'

Rachel's lips twisted in a cynical smile. 'There's more.'

Vivian kept her tone light and raised her cup of cooling coffee to her lips. 'Oh yeah?'

Rachel leaned across the table, her expression conspiratorial. 'My source told me they're as invisible as the Grim Reaper and fart fairy dust.'

Vivian choked on her coffee.

Rachel sat back and watched impassively as she coughed and wiped her mouth with a napkin.

'Fart fairy dust.' Vivian chuckled at the mental image of her team members doing anything that delicate. 'I'm going to have to tell Alex that.'

'Who's Alex?' said Rachel.

Vivian sobered and looked at her steadily. 'Before I answer that question, I need your answer. And the name of your source.'

Rachel narrowed her eyes. 'My source is dead. And the answer is I don't give a damn about your black ops team.'

Too late, Vivian recalled Benjamin Westfield. Westfield had been the leader of Rachel's FAST team in Afghanistan. He had perished in the incident in the Gulf of Aden, along with Tom Cook, another DEA agent. They had both been given closed casket funerals, parts of their mutilated bodies missing, irretrievable from the debris cast into the ocean.

Alex had approached Westfield a year ago, when he was recruiting potential candidates for Division Eight. The DEA agent had refused his offer, citing personal reasons.

Vivian guessed one of those reasons was currently sitting across from her. She took a deep breath while she carefully formulated her next words. As the daughter of a former Chief Justice of the United States, she mingled in social circles that regularly included the political elite of the country and knew how to win them around to her way of thinking, eventually. Still, the light in Rachel's eyes told her she could be on to a losing battle.

'Your psych reports read like something out of a medical textbook on PTSD,' Vivian stated bluntly.

Rachel paled.

'Your boss wants you nowhere near a gun. In fact, last I heard, the very thought of letting you loose in the field was giving him bowel cramps.'

Rachel stiffened in her seat.

Vivian softened her tone. 'Your lover is dead and the future you were looking forward to no longer exists.'

This time, Rachel jumped to her feet, her eyes wild with anger. Behind the rage, Vivian caught a glimpse of a pain so deep her breath caught in her throat.

The only other person in whom she had ever witnessed such soul-deep suffering was Alex.

Although it made her gut twist in self-disgust, Vivian observed Rachel in silence while the latter battled her instinct to knock her teeth out. Judging by what she'd seen in the gym, she was not someone to underestimate in a fight.

Vivian placed her hands flat on the table and looked at Rachel steadily. 'Your field career in the DEA is over. If you don't accept the desk job they're proposing, they'll give you an honorable discharge by the end of the year.' Vivian paused. 'I know what you're capable of. I've seen you in action. And I don't offer such a compliment lightly. I wouldn't be suggesting this position if I didn't think you were the best person to lead EAGLE. This team could be your last chance to carry on doing a job that you love and serve this country to the best of your abilities. I also think Division Eight would be good for you, emotionally.'

Rachel blinked, surprise dampening the anger on her face momentarily before it hardened again.

'EAGLE, huh?' she said, rolling her eyes. 'I suppose yours is "WOLF"?'

Vivian kept her face impassive, rose to her feet, and placed a business card on the table. 'This is my personal number. Give me a ring if you change your mind. And it's ARMOR.'

She made it ten steps to the door before Rachel called out to her.

'Wait.'

❄

CHAPTER FOUR

October 2015. Marrakesh.

Rachel stared at the camera feeds overlaying the satellite image on the computer screen.

'Lea, shift ten degrees east,' she instructed into her wireless transmitter.

One of the feeds panned slightly. The towering, red-brick minaret of Koutoubia Mosque loomed into view, the copper balls atop its spire gleaming under the midday sun. Beneath it and in the foreground, palm trees swayed amid the vivid greenery of a park.

A man in tan Chinos and a loose pink shirt sat reading a paper on a bench some hundred feet from the camera. The Panama hat on his head cast his features in shadows and a watch gleamed brightly against the tanned skin of his forearm.

'Any sign of our contact yet?' said Rachel.

The camera feed moved as Lea Holt, former CIA

undercover operative and one of EAGLE's most versatile assets, shifted from her position. She was currently disguised as a heavy, middle-aged woman in a burka selling fresh orange and grapefruit juice from a compact, portable booth at the edge of the main avenue cutting through the park.

'No. All I'm seeing is the vivid pink of Clint's shirt.'

'Clint?' said Rachel.

The man on the bench crossed his legs and cast a leisurely glance at the path leading toward the mosque before turning a page of the newspaper.

'No,' murmured Clint Brooks into the micro transmitter pinned to the inside collar of his shirt. 'And the color is hot salmon, not pink.'

The former Delta man and Rachel's XO in EAGLE carried on reading the tabloid in his hands, his demeanor that of someone with all the time in the world. The camera in his shirt button showed the other paths leading to the intersection where he sat. The sound of trickling water traveled across the comm line from the fountain twenty feet south of his position.

A sliver of unease danced down Rachel's spine as she watched Clint on Lea's camera feed.

Her gaze switched to one of the other shots. 'Will?'

William King, former Navy SEAL and EAGLE's best sniper, gave her a muttered 'That's a negative,' from his position on the rooftop of a building five hundred feet north-east of the park. 'And Lea is right,' he added. 'You look like a giant candy floss.'

'If either of you lick me, you're dead,' Clint threatened.

Rachel ignored the light banter between her team mates and stared at the feed from the scope cam on Will's rifle, unease turning into apprehension. Even though fifteen hundred feet of hot, bustling city streets separated her from Clint, he seemed to sense her anxiety.

'Relax, Rachel. Our target will show.'

She could almost see his reassuring half-smile in the gloom beneath the Panama hat.

In the eight months they had been working together, a deep friendship had grown between her and the former Delta man Alex Slade had recommended as her second in command. Although Clint could easily have commanded EAGLE himself, he never seemed to begrudge Rachel for taking leadership of the black ops team. Not only did he excel at tactics and logistics, he also helped smooth over the initial rough spots she encountered when she started managing the group of agents and soldiers who made up EAGLE, all of whom were outstanding operatives in their own right. It took a few weeks to get her team working like a well-oiled machine. Now into their tenth mission on foreign soil, they were like family. Family that Rachel would lay her life on the line to protect, like any one of them would.

A lazy Texan drawl came across the comm line. 'Target sighted.'

Rachel's gaze swung to the bottom right feed on the computer screen.

Huck Finn, former U.S. Marine and EAGLE's second-best long-range shooter, sat in the driver's seat of a dusty, black Volvo in the car park to the west of the public garden next to the Koutoubia Mosque. The camera in his sunglasses showed her a brief view of a man in traditional Berber garb striding briskly into the park.

'He's just been dropped off by a white van,' Huck continued in a relaxed tone. 'Plate number is 55531R1.'

Rachel narrowed her eyes. 'That's a Rabat prefecture registration. All team, be advised target is wearing a black djellaba, a kufi cap, and sunglasses. Clint, he'll be at your eight o'clock in twenty seconds. Stay alert, people.'

'Always do,' muttered Will.

'As alive as a woman with an itch,' said Lea.

Silence descended on the comm line.

'For God's sake, Holt, what's with that analogy?' muttered Clint.

'That mental image just burned my retinas,' said Huck.

'You're never going to land a man with that kind of mouth,' said Will.

'What are you, a bunch of Victorian wussies?' said Lea.

Rachel stifled a sigh. Her team still had to learn the subtle nuances of TPO, time, place, and occasion, when it came to their regular comedy routine. A clatter of key strokes sounded at her side, distracting her for a moment.

Pippa Sanderson, former Homeland intelligence and EAGLE's tech lead, typed the number plate Huck had given them into the computer on board the van where she, Rachel, and Barry Eckhart, former U.S.

Marine and EAGLE's weapons and bombs expert, were overseeing the operation. She pushed her glasses up the bridge of her nose and frowned at the dusty boots situated precariously close to her precious workstation. Barry sat on a stool next to hers, feet up on the console table. He ignored her pointed stare. A grimace crossed Pippa's face as she glanced around the interior of the van.

The fluid nature of their mission meant they'd had less than twelve hours to find an appropriate mobile command base for the sting operation currently in play. Compared to the Homeland agent's slick computer lab back at their base outside D.C., the delivery van they had commandeered the night before left a lot to be desired. The air was rich with the smell of caged poultry and bird shit.

The target finally appeared on Clint's camera feed, a growing, dark figure strolling up the path toward the water fountain.

'The van is registered to one Kader Khan,' said Pippa. 'And you were right. The address is listed in Rabat.'

Rachel's gaze remained focused on the figure now visible in three of the feeds on the screen. 'Run the name and address through our databases. Let's see whether anything comes up on the intelligence networks.'

The man in the black djellaba slowed and came to a stop several feet from the bench where Clint sat reading his paper. The former Delta man looked up and slowly lowered the tabloid.

Rachel finally got her first good look at Sasha Yakimov, the target of their mission in Marrakesh. At least, that was their best guess as to his real name.

Known under various guises to intelligence agencies all around the world and on Interpol's top ten most wanted list, the man standing before Clint was a suspected supplier of highly enriched uranium on a growing nuclear black market that was becoming a major cause for concern for the UN Security Council and its member states. With the unstable situation in the Middle East and the rise in terrorist attacks around the world, the Security Council's biggest fear was that dirty bombs, a mixture of conventional explosives and radioactive material, could soon become part of their enemies' arsenal of deadly weapons.

Yakimov was thought to be a significant player in the illicit nuclear trade originating out of Kazakhstan and a key member of an arms and weapons trafficking group with extensive reach across the globe.

It had taken months of deep undercover work by a Mossad agent to identify the man and get close enough to his contacts to arrange the meeting now playing out in the middle of the park next to the Koutoubia Mosque.

'Mr. Smith?' said Yakimov.

Although his name denoted a Russian heritage, Yakimov's nose and high cheekbones reminded Rachel of a young Omar Sharif. She suspected he was built more along the lean lines of Middle-Eastern men than the solid configuration of Russian males behind the cloak that hid his figure. His voice was a surprise, however. Low and mellifluous, it indicated that the speaker was a highly educated and cultured man, in sharp contrast to the crimes he stood accused of.

Pippa brought up the voice stress analysis software on her computer and started recording.

On the screen, Clint folded the paper and put it aside. 'Mr. Yakimov?'

The man in the djellaba smiled and dipped his chin, Clint's figure a bright reflection in his sunglasses. 'May I take a seat?'

'Sure.'

Clint shifted on the bench. Yakimov sat to Clint's left and leaned against the backrest, his posture relaxed. He raised his face to the sun.

'A nice day, is it not?' he said after a pause.

Clint watched him for a moment before looking at the sky. 'It sure is.'

'Hmm,' Pippa murmured.

Rachel dragged her gaze from the video feed and looked at her. 'What is it?'

The former Homeland agent was staring at the voice analysis data on the screen. 'Our man is not as relaxed as he wants us to believe he is.'

Rachel studied the video and satellite feeds. 'Huck, any sign of activity at your end?'

'That's a negative,' murmured the Texan.

'Will?'

'Nothing at my end.'

'Lea?'

There was silence on the comm line.

Rachel narrowed her eyes. 'Lea, do you copy?'

'I do,' came the soft reply.

Rachel straightened. After months of working together with the former CIA operative, she recognized Lea's tone. The agent was onto something.

'What's wrong?'

'You know that itch?'

Rachel frowned. 'What about it?'

'It's getting stronger.'

❄

CHAPTER FIVE

Pippa tensed. Barry lowered his feet off the console, lines furrowing his normally smooth brow.

Every member of their team knew not to disregard Lea's instincts. It had saved them on more than one occasion in the past year.

Yakimov's voice traveled across the wireless receiver in Clint's shirt button. 'My contact tells me you wish to get your hands on some rare goods?'

Clint's cover was that of a mercenary acting on behalf of a buyer of highly enriched uranium from Pakistan. It had taken Pippa several days to set up a convincing front for anyone curious enough to investigate his fake background and history. As it stood, "Mr. Smith" was a highly proficient professional soldier who had worked for some of the biggest drug and arms trafficking organizations in the world.

'I hope you don't mind me saying this, but I do find something rather strange,' said Yakimov. His lips curved in a tiny smile as he continued gazing at the sky.

Clint remained silent, his expression neutral.

'I have been in this business for a long time and yet, up till two weeks ago, I had never heard of the name Smith.'

Yakimov lowered his head and stared at Clint.

The former Delta man smiled faintly. 'Who says Smith is the only name I go by?'

Yakimov grinned. 'Touché. Then, I hope you don't mind explaining why there's a sniper watching us from that building to the north of where we're sitting?'

Rachel's blood turned to ice.

Barry rose to his feet next to her. 'That's not good.'

'Will, watch your back, your position's been compromised,' Rachel said sharply into the wireless transmitter. 'Lea, I want you to extract Clint on my command. Huck, go after Yakimov.'

One of the video feeds changed with dizzying speed as Will rolled behind the cover of a vent and scanned three hundred and sixty degrees around his position through his rifle scope.

Rachel focused on the image from Lea's camera. Clint had not moved.

'Let's just say I'm a very careful guy,' he said, his pose relaxed and a faint smile still playing around his lips.

The grin did not shift from Yakimov's face.

A sliver of hope darted through Rachel. Had their target bought the line her XO had just fed him?

She bit her lip. *If only he'd remove his damn sunglasses.*

You could tell a lot by a man's eyes. And right now, Clint needed to know if Yakimov was playing him or not.

'Interesting,' Yakimov murmured.

'Shit,' said Pippa leadenly.

Rachel glanced at the voice analysis data and felt her gut twist. She recognized the pattern it showed without the Homeland agent having to elaborate further.

'Clint, he's getting ready to—'

The shots came out of nowhere.

Clint jerked twice, as if someone had knocked into his shoulder, and slid off the bench. Yakimov was up and running before her XO's body hit the ground.

Bile rose in Rachel's throat. 'Agent down! I repeat, Clint is—'

'Gotcha!' Will snarled.

Rachel's gaze shifted to the feed from the Navy SEAL's scope cam. In the center of the target sight, a man with a sniper rifle fell from the rooftop of a building south of his position and to the east of the park.

The live satellite feed showed Yakimov nearing the east periphery of the park at a dead run.

'Will, do you have a clear shot?' barked Rachel.

'That's a negative. Too many civvies in the way.'

'Huck, target is approaching the mosque!' she snapped. 'Try and cut him off on the main avenue.'

'Already on it,' said Huck, his normally jovial voice hard.

The Volvo squealed out of the parking lot and

veered onto the busy carriageway south of the mosque. The sound of angry horns came through Huck's receiver as he swerved agilely through the traffic.

Rachel stared at the last camera feed, her heart pounding in her chest. 'Lea?'

The CIA operative had thrown off her burka and rushed to Clint's side. She ripped his shirt open, exposing the slimline body armor beneath it. Relief washed over Rachel when she heard a raspy cough.

Clint blinked and took a shuddering breath. 'Shit, that hurt.'

He rolled onto his side and pushed himself up on an elbow.

'He's going to be all right,' said Lea. 'He took a bullet to the vest, right over the heart. Gonna have himself one nasty bruise. The second bullet went straight through his shoulder.' She slapped some gauze and a pressure bandage into Clint's hand. 'Here! I'm going after the target.'

The view from Lea's camera changed as she jumped to her feet and headed in the direction where Yakimov had disappeared.

'Clint, stay put, we're coming to get you,' Rachel ordered. 'Will, cover him.'

'Like hell you are,' Clint retorted. 'Will, watch our backs. I'm going after that bastard!'

Rachel swallowed a curse as she watched Clint get up and start after Lea on the live satellite feed.

Huck's Volvo came into view near the bottom of the image. The Marine swerved into a one-way road and barreled through a barrage of oncoming traffic toward the intersection opposite the mosque. Yakimov's figure was a dark blur six hundred feet ahead of him.

'Huck's not going to make it.' Barry pointed at the screen. 'Once Yakimov gets through there, we'll lose him.'

Rachel stared from the fleeing figure to the busy road opposite the intersection. It led into the heart of the Medina quarter of the city, a two-square-mile maze of narrow, winding streets and crowded souks packed with tourists and locals. She narrowed her eyes. Barry was right.

'We can cut him off here.' She pointed to an area north of a large marketplace. 'Huck, Yakimov is at your twelve o'clock and heading for the Rue Koutoubia. Lea and Clint are at your nine o'clock and closing. Pippa will guide you from here on. Will, cover us.'

Rachel checked her Sigs and turned to the Homeland agent. 'You're our eyes on the ground. Stay put unless I order you otherwise.'

Pippa nodded, her face set in grim lines.

Rachel was out of the van a second later, Barry on her heels. The hot, humid air hit her like a brick wall as she emerged into a teeming street some thousand feet east of the Koutoubia Mosque. She kept one gun low in hand and sprinted toward the Jemaa El Fna square.

A familiar sound reached her ears above the noise of the city. Gunshots had been fired somewhere to their left.

'Taking fire from multiple unidentified contacts, I repeat, multiple contacts opening fire! Engaging!' Lea shouted in her transmitter.

Clint's voice came over Rachel's earpiece. 'Where the hell did these bastards come from?'

'Don't know, but we're gonna lose the target if we don't get rid of them!' said Huck.

By the sounds of things, the former Marine was on the ground with Lea and Clint.

'Rachel, Barry, Yakimov is four hundred feet at your twelve o'clock,' said Pippa. 'Huck, Lea, and Clint are in Rue Koutoubia. They're being bottled into an alley.'

'Will!' Rachel barked into her transmitter.

'On my way!' said the former SEAL.

Rachel weaved through the sea of bodies filling the busy square, boots pounding the ground. That Yakimov had come prepared for the rendezvous was hardly a surprise; the man had not survived this long without capture by being a trusting fool. What she had not expected was the number of men he had waiting to ambush them, including the sniper. Which meant that, somehow, the details of EAGLE's covert mission in Marrakesh had been leaked to the target.

She scowled. *Worry about that later, Carter. Just concentrate on the mission!*

More gunfire sounded from the west. Some of the locals stopped in their tracks and stared in that direction. A few jumped out of Rachel and Barry's way, their eyes widening when they caught sight of their drawn weapons.

The distant gunfight intensified. Screams rose to the blue skies.

Rachel gritted her teeth. Soon, the fear would

spread, leading to mass panic in the streets and making it easier for Yakimov to disappear.

Not on my goddamned watch!

She reached the other side of the square a heartbeat later and slowed to scan her surroundings, her chest heaving with her breaths and a trickle of sweat running down her back.

Pippa's voice came through the receiver in her ear. 'He's in the alley at your three o'clock!'

Barry spotted the black flash of movement first and was a second ahead of Rachel as they darted into the passageway. She listened to Pippa guiding Will and the others engaging the contacts in Rue Koutoubia with a sinking feeling.

Looks like it'll just be the two of us.

※

CHAPTER SIX

Narrow, thronged alleys lined with shops, stalls, and maze-like bazaars unfolded before them as they headed into the heart of the Medina after Yakimov.

The hot air turned rich with the smell of sweat, fried food, and fragrant spices, the calls of vendors selling their wares rising to the strips of blue sky visible between the buildings crowding the cramped passages. Bemused and angry cries rose from a seemingly endless press of locals and tourists as they were jostled and knocked about by the hunted and hunters charging headlong through them.

Anger distorted Yakimov's features when he looked over his shoulder and saw them gaining ground. He slowed and started knocking people into their path.

Rachel swallowed a curse when several men stumbled into her. She pushed them aside and slipped through the thickening throng, pulse racing, her gaze never leaving Yakimov's fleeing figure.

There was a scuffle and a thud behind her.

She glanced back and saw Barry rolling to his feet, his face set in hard lines as he ignored the shouts of the man and woman who had brought him to the ground.

A loud, metallic clatter sounded in front of her. Rachel looked ahead and saw a kiosk full of copper pots and carafes land three feet from her. She jumped onto a cart, crossed two stalls, and landed on the ground without breaking her stride. Her gaze sought Yakimov once more.

He wasn't there.

Her stomach plummeted. She skidded to a halt at an intersection, scanned the side passages, and saw a wooden door swing shut a dozen feet to her right.

She was through it in seconds. A traditional, tiled Moroccan courtyard dominated by a water fountain and fringed with orange trees and stuccoed arches opened up in front of her.

She barely had time to scan the galleries of the three-story buildings enclosing the open space when a bullet slammed into the terracotta floor next to her foot.

Rachel dove into the cover of a stone pillar. A draft of air warmed the skin on the back of her neck as the door swung open behind her.

She reached out instinctively, grabbed Barry's shirt, and yanked the Marine next to her just as more bullets smashed into the floor and walls close to the column.

She peered past the corner of the archway. A burst of gunfire shattered the air. Rachel pulled back a second before a cloud of stone chips and plaster dust erupted a foot in front of her nose.

'He's on the move on the first floor gallery,' she said in a low voice. 'He's got company. Two tangos on the roof, at twelve and three o'clock.' Her gaze darted to a doorway ten feet to the left. 'Cover me. I'm going after him.'

Barry frowned and opened his mouth. Rachel dashed out from behind the column before he could speak. Bullets flashed past her as she sprinted for the opening. Barry countered, his shots slowing the enemy's gunfire. Then, she was inside the building.

A stairwell opened up in front of her. There was a gasp from the left. Rachel spun around, finger on the trigger of her Sig, blood pounding in her ears. She froze and lowered the gun a fraction. A young woman back-pedaled inside a room, her face deathly pale, two wide-eyed children in tow.

'Barry, watch your fire. We've got civvies in the building.'

'Gotcha.'

The sound of gunshots filled the air around the courtyard as Barry exchanged fire with Yakimov's men. Rachel heard a scream when she reached the first floor gallery. An armed figure fell from the top of the building. She spied Yakimov disappearing up another flight of stairs across the courtyard.

'He's heading for the roof!' she said into her wireless transmitter.

She sprinted up the remaining stairs two steps at a time, barged through a metal door at the top, and dove to the ground.

Bullets plowed the concrete terrace around her. She

rolled, came up on one knee, and took out the gunman at her two o'clock.

She scanned the rooftop. There was no sign of Yakimov.

Rachel dashed to the north end of the terrace, sweat streaming down her face, heart slamming against her ribs. The dizzying rooftop landscape of the Medina opened up before her, a colorful labyrinth of brick, concrete, and corrugated iron.

One floor down, Yakimov raced across the terrace atop an adjacent building. Rachel took several steps back, ran, and jumped across the narrow alley separating her from her prey.

Yakimov looked around at the sound of her boots landing solidly on the rooftop. He had lost his sunglasses during the chase. She glimpsed panic in his dark eyes as she rushed toward him. He turned and dropped from view.

Rachel staggered to a halt at the edge of the roof. A quiet passage opened up below. Yakimov was climbing down the series of narrow, metal balconies dotting the north wall of the building. She followed, her steps surefooted and her movements nimble as she leapt and swung her way toward the ground.

She reached the alley a couple of seconds behind him. Yakimov was already running toward a busy intersection thirty feet to the west. She straightened, steadied her breath, took out her Sig, and raised it. She fired a single shot.

The bullet caught Yakimov in the side of his left thigh. He cried out, stumbled against a wall, and turned around. There was a gun in his hand. She walked steadily toward him and fired again.

Her second shot knocked the weapon out of his hand and took off his little finger. A bellow of pain and rage left his lips. Undaunted, he whipped a dagger out of his cloak and charged toward her. Rachel holstered the Sig, slipped her Kbar out of her thigh sheath, and countered his strike as he swung his blade at her.

Despite his wounds, Yakimov was skilled with a knife. His dagger whispered within kissing distance of her flesh twice as they stabbed, blocked, and parried in a lethal dance of blades. She got two slashes across his hand and chest before a bullet slammed into his right shoulder. He cursed, arm going limp at his side.

Rachel turned. Barry was running down the alley toward her, gun in hand. His eyes widened. He opened his mouth to shout something, his pace quickening.

She felt movement behind her, ducked, and brought her blade up as she twisted on her heels. Another shot shattered the air just as her knife entered Yakimov's abdomen where he loomed behind her, one hand raised to drive his blade into her back.

A bullet slammed into the back of Yakimov's right leg, bringing him to his knees. He fell onto his side, a grunt escaping his pale lips, his hands clasping the bloody wound in his stomach.

Rachel looked up and saw a figure outlined against the skyline atop a building some two hundred feet across the intersection. She rose to her feet.

'You do realize we need this guy alive, right?' she said into her transmitter.

'I'm sorry,' said Will. 'My finger slipped.'

She turned and stared pointedly at Barry as he came to a stop next to her.

The Marine shrugged. 'As far as I can see, you're the one who inflicted the potentially deadly wound here. Will and I aimed for his limbs.'

Rachel studied the groaning man at their feet, feeling somewhat contrite. Barry was right, as usual.

Footsteps sounded to the left. She looked around. The rest of the cavalry had arrived. Barry squatted and started applying first aid to the bleeding Yakimov.

'What'd we miss?' said Lea.

Clint scowled. 'Is he dead?'

'Whoa, that's a lot of blood.' Huck stared. 'Who knifed him?'

❄

CHAPTER SEVEN

The order came four hours later, as dusk fell across the land.

Rachel paced the corridor outside the recovery room where Yakimov lay sedated following his surgery. Her nails bit into her palms. She resisted the urge to barge inside the chamber and put another bullet into him.

The Mossad agent who had infiltrated the group Yakimov belonged to had been found dead three hours ago in an abandoned warehouse owned by Kader Khan, the man who had driven their target to the rendezvous point at the Koutoubia Mosque. The agent had been tortured almost beyond recognition before being executed with a bullet to the head.

It seemed his cover was compromised when Yakimov's men taped one of his phone conversations during the routine surveillance they carried out on new additions to the group. Khan himself revealed this to the Moroccan intelligence agency after spending forty minutes in a locked cell with two of the Mossad agent's colleagues.

The death of an operative, any operative, was something all intelligence agencies took to heart. Although Rachel knew that what had happened was beyond her control, guilt still twisted through her at the thought of what the man she had never met had gone through in his final moments.

Her only consolation lay in the fact that he had not died needlessly. EAGLE's mission was a success and Yakimov was now in their custody, along with several of his men.

'Here, take this,' someone said behind her.

Rachel turned and eyed the cup of coffee Clint held toward her. His left arm was in a sling. The outline of a pressure bandage was visible over his shoulder.

'It'll keep your hands busy,' said Lea.

She lay on a row of chairs alongside the wall, eyes closed and hands folded neatly under her ribcage. Will slept on the opposite row, the military cap covering his face muffling his snores.

Rachel hesitated before taking the cup off Clint.

He indicated a chair. 'Sit.'

She cocked an eyebrow, irritation darting through her. 'You're being very bossy.'

Clint sighed. 'Right now, you look like you're thinking of doing something stupid.' He glanced around. 'Need I remind you that we're not on American soil?'

'We ain't visiting if your ass ends up in a Moroccan jail,' Lea added.

Rachel frowned and took the seat. Clint dropped down next to her.

'Pippa's decoded the encrypted files on the computer Moroccan police seized at Khan's address,' he said in a low voice. 'Seems the UN task force was right. The uranium was traveling through a French industrial company to a front venture in the United Arab Emirates. The money was paid into the UAE company's Dutch bank in Dubai before making its way to France via Spain.'

Rachel took a sip of the hot, pungent drink. She grimaced at the bitter taste. 'Is there enough there to nail the rest of the group?'

Clint shrugged. 'She's not sure. But it's a solid start.'

Rachel closed her eyes and dropped her head against the cool, concrete wall. 'The Mossad agent. Did he have a family?'

She felt Clint's gaze on her face in the silence that followed. 'His parents died when he was twelve. He had a brother.' Clint paused. 'He was getting married in December.'

Rachel clenched her jaw, a wave of familiar emotion washing over her. Images flashed across her inner vision from that fateful night sixteen months ago, when her whole world had turned upside down in a bright flare of heat and light. Though time had numbed the pain of losing the man she loved and one of her FAST team members, the nightmares still came at least once a week. Moments like these brought the agony of her loss all too sharply into focus once more.

'Rachel?'

She opened her eyes and looked into her XO's concerned face. 'I'm fine.'

Clint looked unconvinced. He was the only member of EAGLE who knew what had happened and how much she had lost the night Benjamin died in the Gulf of Aden. It was Vivian Thorpe who had advised her to talk to him.

'As team leader and XO, you need to have the utmost trust in each other, even if it means exposing the skeletons in your closets,' Vivian told her a few weeks after she took over EAGLE.

Though she had dreaded having the conversation, talking to Clint had turned out to be strangely cathartic. For the first time since she woke up after the explosion, Rachel felt she had someone to share the burden of her pain with. And Clint did not let the admission affect their working relationship; he was a hard task master and challenged her without fail whenever their opinions differed.

Footsteps rose from the east end of the corridor. Pippa approached briskly, satellite phone in hand. Barry strolled a few steps behind her.

'Where's Huck?' said Clint.

Pippa sighed. 'Where else would he be?'

'He's making moon eyes at some poor woman somewhere on the base, isn't he?' murmured Lea.

'Bingo,' said Pippa. She handed the satellite phone to Rachel. 'There's a phone call for you. It's from Washington.'

Rachel took the phone, curious; she had already

updated the UN task force leader on the outcome of their mission.

'There's a Lockheed Hercules fueling up outside,' said Alex Slade at the other end of the line. 'I want your team on it in thirty minutes.'

Rachel went still. 'What's this about?'

Lea opened her eyes and straightened in her chair, her expression suddenly focused. Barry nudged Will's shoulder. The former SEAL took the cap off his face, blinked, and sat up.

Rachel felt EAGLE's eyes on her as she waited for Alex's reply.

'I'll tell you when you get there,' he said in clipped tones.

She frowned and glanced toward Yakimov's room. 'Our directive was to secure—'

'I've got agents from the FBI's Legal Attaché office in Rabat on their way to you now. They'll babysit Yakimov until he's well enough to be extradited.' He paused. 'This is a top priority mission, Rachel. I want complete communication blackout until you hear from me.'

'Can you at least tell me where we're—?'

The dial tone echoed in Rachel's ear. She lowered the phone and stared at it. She had never known Alex Slade to be fazed by anything. Whatever was going down had to be bad.

'Get Huck.'

❈

They landed at a military airport at daybreak, some ten hours later. The thread of tension that had been dancing along Rachel's nerves since Alex hung up on her tightened further when the loading doors of the Hercules opened. She had thought she recognized the outlines of the Air Force base under the lightening sky when the plane was making its final approach. She was now certain of their location.

It was where she had been airlifted sixteen months ago, after the disastrous events in the Gulf of Aden.

They exited the aircraft and made their way to the Jeep escorts waiting on the tarmac.

'Anyone know where the hell this is?' said Huck.

'We're thirty miles southeast of Addis Ababa,' Rachel muttered.

Huck's steps faltered. 'We're in *Ethiopia?*'

'Keep up,' said Clint curtly as they neared the Jeeps.

Two taciturn officers wearing the uniforms of the Ethiopian Air Force drove them to a brightly-lit hangar some thousand feet from the runway. They disappeared in a squeal of tires the second EAGLE got out of the Jeeps.

Rachel watched the vehicles' taillights fade into the distance before studying the building. A UH-1N Huey helicopter sat to the left of the open hangar doors, next to two mud-streaked trucks and four SUVs. By the looks of the aircraft and the vehicles, they had all seen recent gunfire. To the right, a team of military medical personnel attended to a group of injured soldiers wearing the uniform of the Ethiopian Army Ground Forces.

Squatting in the middle of the hangar, and looking as incongruous as a wedding dress at a funeral, was a large, shiny, black shipping container on the back of a semi-trailer truck.

'Well, the weirdness factor just went up a notch,' Huck said leadenly.

A door opened in the side of the container. A man wearing tactical gear stepped down a metal ladder and crossed the floor toward them. He was six foot one, with light, short-cropped brown hair and steel-blue eyes that were dark with some unfathomable emotion. Dried blood stained the tanned skin over his right temple and the fresh scrapes on the knuckles of his hands.

'Follow me,' he said coolly.

He turned and retraced his steps.

Rachel studied him for a heartbeat before heading after his disappearing figure, EAGLE in tow.

Whoever this man is, he's used to being in charge.

❇

CHAPTER EIGHT

'Thirty-six hours ago, Melissa Hunt, the daughter of U.S. Vice President Alan Hunt, was kidnapped from a secure compound in the center of Addis Ababa by a group of fifteen armed men. The U.S. Secret Service bodyguards assigned to her detail were killed during the assault.'

Rachel's pulse jumped. Clint drew a sharp breath beside her. She focused on Alex Slade's voice over the video satellite link from D.C., her gaze never leaving the large, flat-screen monitor on the wall at the head of the room.

Security camera recordings showing the incident he had described played in separate windows across it, the brutal reality of the event rendered stark by the silent black and white images.

They were inside a SCIF, a soundproof chamber designed for handling sensitive, classified information relating to national security matters that required the utmost secrecy and could never be made public. Used by the U.S. and other governments and agencies around the world, a portable version of the compartment could be transported to and set up on a temporary command site on the ground, in the air, or at sea.

Or, in this instance, the back of a shipping container in the middle of an Air Force base in North Africa.

'A media black out was instituted by the White House within an hour of the incident,' said Alex. 'No one apart from Director Caldwell, the President, the Vice President, and the National Security Advisor know that Melissa Hunt is currently in the hands of suspected terrorists. Hence why we're using the SCIF.' He paused. 'No need to emphasize that the rule of plausible deniability applies to this mission and everything I'm telling you. As far as the Ethiopian government is concerned, the abduction attempt was unsuccessful and Melissa Hunt is currently on her way back to the United States under diplomatic escort.'

Rachel frowned.

'WOLF was assigned the task of rescuing the Vice President's daughter under the guise of tracking the group responsible for the failed kidnapping,' Alex continued.

Rachel startled. *WOLF? You're kidding me.*

She glanced at the strangers in the SCIF, her gaze settling last on the man who had greeted them in the hangar. He met her stare head-on.

Apart from ARMOR, the first Division Eight team,

Rachel did not know how many other teams existed in the section, or their code names.

'WOLF used data from the GPS devices Melissa Hunt was carrying and tracked her location to the Harenna Forest,' said Alex. 'Eleven hours ago, they attempted a rescue mission with the assistance of Ethiopian Army Ground Forces.' He hesitated. 'They were unsuccessful. Not only did the group behind this kidnapping get away with the Vice President's daughter, they also captured Tristan Payne, WOLF's second in command.'

'Holy shit,' whispered Huck.

'Hang on,' said Rachel. 'Why Division Eight? This is a job for military special ops.'

The man with the steel-blue eyes stirred on the other side of the table. She glanced at him and caught the glint of anger in his gaze. She wasn't sure whom it was directed at.

A muscle jumped in Alex's jaw when he spoke. 'WOLF was on its way back from a mission in Egypt.'

A buzzing sound filled Rachel's ears at his words. *This is like the Gulf of Aden all over again.*

'They were the closest black ops team in the region,' she stated, clamping down on the wave of nausea rising from the pit of her stomach.

'Yes,' said Alex. 'I convinced Director Caldwell that WOLF could carry out this mission.' His gaze shifted to the man across the table from Rachel. 'I still stand by that conviction, Jason. We have reason to believe details of your operation were leaked to the enemy in the hour before your assault on the compound in the

Bale Mountains. What took place in the Harenna Forest would have happened even if SEALs or Marine Special Ops were in charge of the rescue attempt.'

Rachel felt Clint's anxious gaze on her.

She gave him a reassuring glance, took a deep breath, and addressed the man across the table. 'Talk me through it.'

❄

JASON DAVID SCOTT III CLENCHED HIS TEETH AND gazed steadily back at the woman opposite him.

As a general rule of thumb, the Division Eight teams did not know of each other's existence, nor did they interact with one another. This was not exactly a taboo; it was just the nature of Division Eight itself and team dynamics. When Alex Slade recruited him from the U.S. Rangers two years ago to lead WOLF, the second Division Eight team to be created after ARMOR, it was with the promise that he would only be accountable to himself, Director Caldwell, and the President. He would have free reign over how he ran his missions and could select his team members from the pool of candidates Alex screened as suitable for the position.

Running WOLF was the most challenging yet most rewarding job Jason had had since he left the shadow of his wealthy New Hampshire family and his senator father to join the U.S. Army twelve years ago. Although he enjoyed his time in the Ranger Regiment, he always knew he was made for bigger and better things. When opportunity came knocking in the shape of Alex Slade, he jumped at the chance to lead his own elite black ops team and do even more for his country.

Up until eleven hours ago, WOLF had had a one hundred per cent mission success rate. This was their first failure in two years of working together. And the stark weight of the disastrous events of last night was visible on the face of every member of his team. He stopped himself from glancing at the empty space beside him.

Not every team member.

Tristan Payne was more than just his XO. He was also a former U.S. Ranger and Jason's best friend from the age of five. The agony of losing the man he considered his brother was a deep and bitter wound twisting through his soul.

Rachel Carter raised an eyebrow at him as a protracted silence filled the room. Jason knew why she was here. It didn't mean he had to like it.

'Melissa Hunt had three GPS devices on her.' He rubbed the knuckles of his left hand absent-mindedly. 'The kidnappers stripped her of her clothes, shoes, and jewelry when they took her at the secure compound in Addis Ababa, so we lost the traces from her shoe and watch. It was the implanted tracker in her abdomen that led us to her location in the Harenna Forest. The enemy's stronghold was inside a system of caves deep inside the Bale Mountains. We used thermal remote sensing to identify a back way into the mountain, infiltrated the area without detection, and were inside the caves when—'

He stopped and glanced at the grim faces around him. 'It seems clear now that they were expecting us. They came at us from the front and the rear, in a classic pincer move. Tristan was in the lead. They threw stun grenades and grabbed him before any of us could get to him. We went after them but they used RPGs to blast the tunnels closed. By the time we dug our way out of the caves, they were long gone. We lost six Ethiopian soldiers during the assault.'

'Why didn't they just kill Payne?' said one of the EAGLE team members, a woman with shoulder-length brown hair and glasses. She blinked at the battery of hostile stares that suddenly came her way. 'I'm just saying,' she muttered.

'A special ops soldier is a precious commodity, Pippa,' said Rachel. 'He's worth more to them alive than dead. Plus, they can try to extract useful intelligence information from him to sell to the highest bidder.'

Jason stiffened. 'Tristan would never betray his team. Or his country.'

'I'm not saying he would.' Rachel ignored his scowl and turned to the video satellite link. 'Any idea who this group is and what they want?'

Alex watched her for a silent beat across the transatlantic link. 'There is some indication they could be affiliated to the drug cartel behind the capture of the *Nostradamus* last year. As to their demand, it came in an hour ago. They want $30 million delivered to an account in Zurich by oh six hundred hours tomorrow or they will broadcast the execution of Melissa Hunt and Tristan Payne live on the Internet.'

CHAPTER NINE

RACHEL'S BREATH FROZE IN HER THROAT. SHE DROPPED her hands below the table and curled her fingers into the fabric of her trousers.

She was surprised at the steadiness of her voice when she could finally speak. 'Are you sure about the *Nostradamus* connection?'

'The intel coming in is pretty convincing,' Alex replied.

'The *Nostradamus*?' Jason narrowed his eyes. 'Isn't that the cargo ship that was taken by pirates over a year ago in the Gulf of Aden? The one where a couple of DEA agents and a Marine lost their lives?'

'Yes, it is,' said Alex. 'We don't know why or how Melissa Hunt became the target of this cartel. Although they're involved in human trafficking, kidnapping high-profile foreign nationals for ransom is not exactly part of their MO. We won't know their motive unless we capture them.'

'What was the VP's daughter doing in this part of the world?' said Clint.

'She volunteered for a VSO education program in Addis Ababa after finishing her studies at Yale University,' said one of the WOLF members, a woman with short dark hair and piercing brown eyes.

'She was teaching kids?' said Clint.

'Yeah,' muttered another WOLF member, a skinny guy with blond hair and green eyes. 'Her father insisted she have trackers before he let her anywhere near the African continent.'

Rachel digested this information in silence. The irony of being back in East Africa, possibly chasing the same group who had been behind the death of her fiancé, was not lost on her. Just as she was getting her life back together, it seemed Fate was determined to throw down a gauntlet.

Sink or swim, Carter.

Clint shifted beside her. Rachel could practically feel the wave of concern rolling off him. She took a shallow breath and gritted her teeth.

I didn't sink the last time you threw me into the ocean. I sure ain't about to start now.

'I take it you assigned us here to help WOLF rescue Melissa Hunt and Tristan Payne?' she asked Alex.

He nodded. 'Yes. But I want you to be the lead on the mission this time.'

Shocked silence filled the room. Rachel blinked, uncertain she had heard his words correctly.

Jason's voice turned steely. 'Come again?'

Something drew Alex's attention away from the camera.

'Excuse me.'

A woman appeared in the periphery of the feed and passed him a note before disappearing. His eyes narrowed as he read it.

'I'm gonna have to leave you,' he said abruptly, looking back into the camera. 'We're in the middle of a tactical operation right now and I'm needed on the ground.'

Rachel noticed his haggard appearance for the first time.

ARMOR's team leader looked like he had hardly slept in the last twenty-four hours.

'We've already faced these combatants once and we've been on the ground for nearly twenty-four hours,' said Jason. He glanced at Rachel. 'I'm more than happy for EAGLE to assist us in this mission but I feel I should—'

Alex rose to his feet and leaned toward the camera.

'Jason, this is not a judgment on your leadership skills,' he said in a hard voice. 'If the situation were reversed, I would want you to take over Rachel's command.' He sighed and ran a hand through his hair. 'I know what Tristan means to you and I know you will move Heaven and Earth to get the bastards who took him and the Vice President's daughter. But you're far too emotionally invested in this mission and you may not be able to make decisions with a cool head. We need someone detached from the situation to do that.'

His gaze shifted. 'Rachel, you're team leader for both WOLF and EAGLE as of this moment. Get back to me when you have more intel.'

The satellite link blinked out.

Rachel stared at the dark feed for a moment before examining the disgruntled faces on the other side of the table. The enormity of the responsibility she had just been given weighed down on her, a shackle she had not asked for and did not want.

She glanced at Clint and the rest of EAGLE. The confidence in their eyes calmed her ruffled nerves.

'Look, I don't like this any more than you do.' She studied the hostile expressions on the other side of the room. 'I don't know you and I don't know Tristan Payne. But one thing I am certain of. If we don't work together on this and do it like we mean it, then your friend will die, along with the Vice President's daughter. Maybe even other people in this room.'

The animosity level dropped a notch. A muscle jumped in Jason's cheek. He turned to look at his team.

'Carter is right. We're running out of time and we sure as hell can't engage in a "who'll blink first" competition. I want to save Tristan and Melissa. Are you in?'

'Of course we're in,' snapped the woman with the short dark hair. 'It's just—' She glanced at Rachel. 'It seems risky changing our team's dynamics in the middle of a mission.'

'What Jess is saying makes sense,' said a man built like a tank. He cocked a thumb toward EAGLE.

'Besides, these guys are fresh meat. They've been around what, six months?'

'It's been eight,' said Huck. The Marine was grinning. Or, at least, he had exposed his teeth. 'Want to try me out? See what I'm made of?'

'Huck,' Clint murmured.

'Anytime, anywhere,' said the tank.

Oh boy, thought Rachel. She glanced at Jason. He rolled his eyes.

In that moment, she felt a strange connection with the man whose team she had just taken over. She smiled. He blinked, something like surprise flashing on his face.

Rachel rose to her feet.

'Let's take five and get some fresh air,' she said in a firm voice. 'I'm kind of drowning in testosterone right now and some of you don't smell so sharp after your mission. After that, we'll go over what we know so far over breakfast and coffee.'

※

'What did you find at the compound in Addis Ababa?' said Clint.

'Not a whole damn lot,' said Jason.

They were studying the security feeds from the primary incident where Melissa Hunt was taken.

'We have no voice recordings that could help us identify who these guys are,' said Zac Park, the thin guy with the blond hair and green eyes. He was former CIA and WOLF's tech lead. 'Plates on their SUVs were obviously fake. There are no CCTV cameras in the city or on the highways that could help us identify their current or past location even if we knew the real number plates.'

'This was a very slick operation,' said Jason. 'They were in and out of there in under fifteen minutes. They'd obviously been planning this for months.'

'What about DNA? Any of them get injured at the compound?' said Lea.

'Not that we can see on the security feeds or from witness accounts,' said Jessica Powers. She was former Navy Intelligence and in charge of WOLF's tactics and logistics with Tristan Payne.

'There was that much blood from the U.S. Secret Service agents, it would take time to identify any from the kidnappers,' said Edison Barnes, former FBI and WOLF's sniper.

Rachel frowned. 'And there was absolutely no indication from local or regional intel that there was a potential threat to Melissa Hunt's life?'

'None,' said Claire Parsons. The former undercover operative had been at the CIA training grounds a year before Lea. 'We've got agents from the FBI Legal Attaché office in Addis Ababa interrogating eye witnesses.'

'Staff working at the compound?' said Lea.

Claire nodded. 'They've all been cleared.'

'The guys who led the assault had Beretta M9 and Px4 Storm pistols, as well as Heckler & Koch assault rifles,' said Dustin Tate, the guy built like a tank. He was a former SEAL and WOLF's weapons and bombs expert. 'Same thing in the caves in Harenna. They were using new RPGs and even had a couple of MK153 Mod 2s, the latest Shoulder Launched Multi-Purpose Assault Weapon.'

Barry raised an eyebrow. 'Not exactly cheap.'

'Nor easily available on the black market,' said Jessica. 'From what we've seen of them in action, these guys are extremely well trained and well funded.'

Jason turned to Rachel. 'Does this match the intel about the East African drug cartel?'

Rachel shifted under his piercing blue gaze. Now that he had accepted her as the lead on WOLF's current mission, the former Ranger no longer displayed the subtle air of anger and defiance he had projected when they first met. Rachel wasn't so sure this was a good thing. A relaxed Jason Scott was proving somewhat distracting.

'The group who took the *Nostradamus* were similarly trained and had military grade weapons,' she replied in a steady voice. 'What we know of their activities in the Horn of Africa corroborates this.'

'And no one's been able to place an undercover operative inside the cartel?' said Jessica.

'No.' Rachel hesitated. 'DEA tried once. The agent was found dead two weeks after making contact with them.'

'You said there was a tracker inside Melissa Hunt,' said Clint. 'Is it still transmitting?'

Jason's expression hardened. 'It did for half an hour after the assault in the Harenna Forest. The last time we picked up a signal was ten miles east of the caves.'

Rachel's stomach plummeted. The meaning behind his words was all too clear.

'They cut it out of her?' she said quietly.

Jason nodded, the anger darkening his features matching the indignation coursing through her and the rest of EAGLE.

'You find anything in Harenna that might give us a clue as to the identities or motives of the men who did this?' said Lea.

'No,' said Jason. 'We have diggers at the tunnels right now but by the time we excavate down to the caves and complete a search, the deadline will have expired.'

Rachel's gaze shifted to the frozen images of the Addis Ababa security feeds. *We don't have a whole lot to go on.*

'What about your body cams? I know you wouldn't have been able to upload live to the server from those caves, but have you looked at them?'

Ever since Alex Slade got framed and almost ended up in jail for treason a few years ago, all Division Eight team members were now required to wear body cameras during an active mission, however sensitive the operation. There had been occasions when the recordings yielded precious intel the human eye had not registered at the time.

Jessica frowned. 'Yes. I've been over the data several times.'

'A fresh pair of eyes wouldn't hurt,' Rachel said steadily.

The former Naval Intelligence officer hesitated before dipping her chin.

They spent the next half hour studying the recordings she had uploaded to one of the secure Division Eight servers in the U.S. The last video was the one from Jason's body camera.

Jessica forwarded the clip to after the team had entered the tunnel that would lead them to the caves. On the screen, Tristan Payne negotiated the passage carefully, his figure stark in the ghostly green light of the camera's night vision. Twenty minutes into the mission, brightness flared across the screen, just after he turned a corner.

Though she had heard it several times in the other WOLF members' videos, the boom of the flash bang grenade still startled Rachel.

Jason fell against the wall, a curse escaping his lips. Smoke filled the camera's viewfinder. He shouted Tristan's name, pushed himself off, and staggered forward. More flashes and bangs followed, drowning the staccato of assault rifles. Despite the fact that the grenades must have disorientated WOLF, they responded to the enemy's fire with cold efficiency. Edison joined Jason. The two men advanced swiftly down the passage, determination evident in their every step.

Seconds later, an explosion brought down the walls and ceiling ahead of them. Something twisted inside Rachel's chest when Jason shouted Tristan's name once more. She had not heard the desperation in his voice in the other recordings.

She watched the static on the feed for several seconds before turning to Jessica. 'You're right. There's nothing there.'

'Have you looked for geospatial intelligence?' said Clint. 'Were there any reconnaissance or commercial satellites in the sky that could have captured the enemy's escape route?'

'You would have thought so, but no,' said Zac. 'By the time they left the cover of the trees, that particular area of the Harenna Forest was no longer in the target field of any overhead cameras. NGA wouldn't give us a dedicated window and we couldn't get a UAV in the air in time for the op.'

Frustration gnawed at Rachel's insides. She glanced at the clock on the monitor. It was now oh eight hundred hours. They had less than a day left to locate and save Melissa Hunt and Tristan Payne.

That is, if they are even still alive.

She was chiding herself for this dark thought when a knock sounded on the SCIF's secure door. Jason left his seat and opened it.

An Ethiopian Army officer stood on the other side. 'There's an urgent call for you.'

Jason stepped out.

Rachel rose and walked over to the map of Ethiopia fixed to the wall. 'We should concentrate our efforts on Addis Ababa. Get the FBI to check local sources. They might have missed some intel that could—'

The SCIF door opened forcefully. Jason stormed in,

an odd expression on his face. It took a moment for Rachel to read the excitement in his eyes. Her pulse accelerated.

'An Ethiopian soldier found something outside the caves in Harenna.'

The whole room leaned forward.

'It's Tristan's body camera.'

❄

CHAPTER TEN

Fuck, fuck, fuck!

Tristan kept his face carefully blank as he looked across the room. Fifteen feet away, Melissa Hunt lay on a camp bed, sweat and blood from a cut in her forehead streaking her pale face. She gritted her teeth and winced as a masked man changed the dressing on her abdomen. Two men with HK416 assault rifles stood by the door, their eyes on Tristan.

Twelve hours had passed since his capture in the caves in the Harenna Forest. He still cursed the moment three men had jumped him inside the tunnel. By the time he recovered from the flash bang grenade they lobbed at him, they had struck him on the head with the butt of a rifle. The ensuing gunfight between WOLF and the masked men behind the abduction of the VP's daughter had given him hope they would be rescued imminently. The explosions that brought the tunnel walls down minutes later killed that prospect.

It was obvious to him now that the enemy had been waiting for them.

Admiration darted through the former Ranger as he studied the Vice-President's daughter. Melissa had shown a depth of courage he would not have thought possible of someone from one of the most powerful families in the world. Though he knew little about the twenty-three-year-old apart from the basic profile WOLF had been given at the start of their mission, there was no denying that she was a survivor.

He would never forget the moment two men held her down while a third cut the GPS tracker out of her body when they were traveling in the back of a van after the failed rescue mission. Her screams had filled the small space and brought a red haze of fury across Tristan's vision. He had yelled and cursed as he struggled against the bonds around his wrists and ankles. All that had done was earn him another beating.

Luckily, the device had been located just beneath her skin. They had glued and dressed her wound before bundling the two prisoners into the back of a helicopter. With his head covered by a canvas bag, Tristan had been unable to see which direction they flew in. From the sound of the rotors, he guessed the aircraft to be a Sikorsky UH-60. The trip lasted just over three hours.

The door of their prison opened, distracting him. A man with blue eyes and a shaved head walked in. He was not wearing a mask.

'How is she?' he asked coldly in Afrikaans.

'The wound was superficial,' said the masked man tending to Melissa. 'I've given her a shot of antibiotic just in case.'

'Good. We wouldn't want her to die from an infection.' The man whom Tristan now knew to be the leader of the group who had abducted Melissa and killed her bodyguards turned and studied him. His brawny build and the way he walked screamed professional soldier. 'What about him?'

The masked man rose to his feet and took off his bloodied gloves. 'Couple of broken ribs and a dislocated shoulder. Nothing permanent.'

Tristan looked up as the mercenary walked over and towered over him.

'Which special ops team do you belong to?'

Tristan smiled and ignored the stinging pain shooting across his swollen face. They had asked him the question a dozen times since they captured him.

He tried a new variation on his answers. 'The seven dwarfs.'

The mercenary grinned. Pain exploded in Tristan's gut as the man's boot connected viciously with his abdomen.

He gagged and coughed before gasping out, 'The Tin Man's army!'

A low chuckle sounded from across the room. The mercenary turned and looked at Melissa.

'Kermit's Green Berets,' she said.

Another wave of respect washed over Tristan at the defiant light blazing in her hazel eyes.

'The Peanuts gang,' he mumbled.

She gave him a quizzical look.

He suddenly felt older than his thirty-two years. 'Before your time.'

The mercenary stared. 'Don't worry. You'll talk.'

Tristan read the threat in his eyes before he left the room with the masked men in tow. The former Ranger knew he would be lucky to make it out of there alive. And there was little prospect Melissa Hunt would survive this ordeal either.

Their only hope lay with the body camera he had knocked off his tactical gear when he was struggling against his captors outside the caves in the Harenna Forest.

That's if somebody finds it.

He had just gotten his breath back when heavy footsteps sounded outside their cell. The door slammed open. The mercenary stormed back in with five of his men. A sick feeling twisted through Tristan when he saw what they held in their hands.

Melissa's eyes widened. She rolled on her side and started to sit up.

The mercenary signaled to his men. Two of them strode to the bed, yanked the young woman's arms above her head and pulled her feet apart, pinning her to the mattress.

'It looks like your government doesn't quite understand we mean business.' The mercenary stared at Tristan. 'Division Eight, is it?'

Tristan's stomach plummeted. *How the hell did he find out?*

'Seems your people in Washington decided to send

some help. Another Division Eight team landed in Ethiopia a couple of hours ago.' The mercenary strolled to the bed and stood towering above the struggling woman, his face impassive. 'Let's show them how serious we can get.'

'Don't do this,' Tristan said in a low voice, heart pounding and acid burning his throat.

Melissa glanced at him, her eyes dark with fear.

'Don't worry,' the mercenary told Tristan. 'I haven't forgotten about you.'

The men flipped Melissa onto her front. A muffled cry left her lips as they forced her face into the pillow. The mercenary leaned down and ripped the shirt off her back.

❄

CHAPTER ELEVEN

'Thanks for doing this, Bob,' said Jessica. 'Can you get the camera to us afterward?'

'Sure. I'm flying to the capital in the next hour. I'll drop it off on the way.'

Jessica ended the video call and logged onto another site.

Bob Kendall, an FBI agent from the Addis Ababa field office, was on site in the Harenna Forest. He had taken Tristan's body camera in as evidence. With the deadline looming, they could not afford to have him bring it to them from where it had been found, two hundred miles away. On Jessica's instruction, he had uploaded the data to an agency server she could access.

The video was soon up and running. Jessica forwarded the clip to fifteen minutes into the mission. Tristan's capture came moments later, with the now familiar sight and sound of the flash bang grenade.

Whiteness filled the viewer of his body camera. A shadow swooped down from above. There was a thud and a grunt. Gunfire erupted in the background as WOLF engaged the enemy.

The smoke from the grenade gradually cleared. The image from Tristan's body camera changed to the floor of the tunnel and the boots of his captors as he was dragged half-conscious along the ground. Explosions followed. The rumble of the tunnel caving in echoed from the monitor's speakers.

They heard Tristan moan. The perspective changed as he stumbled and struggled to his feet. His captors came into view.

Rachel leaned forward and studied the screen. The men all wore ski masks. Their eyes shone eerily in the camera's night vision. They shouted at Tristan in Afrikaans and forced him into a brightly-lit cave.

'Is there enough there for voice analysis?' said Rachel.

'I doubt it,' said Zac.

'I agree,' murmured Pippa.

Through the chaotic jumble of images that followed, Rachel glimpsed crates of ammunitions lining the walls of the cavern. WOLF's assumption had been correct. The people behind Melissa Hunt's abduction were no amateurs.

Tristan and his captors entered another system of tunnels.

Clint straightened.

'Is that—?'

Some fifteen feet ahead, a group of men were hurrying along the passage. A slender figure with her hands tied behind her back swam in and out of view among them, arms gripped by a couple of masked figures. At one point, she struggled against her captors and glanced over her shoulder.

Jessica froze the clip. They stared at the screen.

'Well, at least we know she was alive and well up till then,' said Lea.

Although she was gagged and the image was in the infrared spectrum, it was clearly Melissa Hunt on the video feed.

'Keep going,' said Jason in a hard voice.

They watched as Tristan was manhandled through more caves and tunnels after Melissa and the other men. The sounds of a gunfight grew in the distance. Then they were outside the mountain.

The camera's night vision caught the flash of muzzles from the Ethiopian Army ground forces engaging the men guarding the caves. The sounds of the fierce battle were overshadowed by the sudden whistles and explosions of RPGs. Bright light flared across the viewfinder. The gunfire died down.

There was a scuffle as Tristan started fighting his captors. He stumbled against one of the men. The body camera was knocked to the ground. Tristan's boot came into view. He kicked the device out of the way. It spun in the dirt before coming to rest against a rock, giving them a wide-angled view of the area outside the caves.

Another thud and grunt followed as Tristan was struck in the back of the head with the butt of a rifle. His captors caught him as he fell. Head lolling, he was hauled semi-conscious toward three vans parked under the trees some twenty feet away. They dumped him into the back of the first vehicle. Engines rumbled into life. The men piled into the vans and rolled out into the darkness.

The sounds of the forest rose from the speakers in the aftermath of their departure, trees rising starkly against the night sky in the camera's night vision. Jessica stopped the video.

'Go back ten seconds,' said Rachel.

Jessica rewound the clip and froze it.

'Well, we got a partial plate,' said Clint.

Rachel studied the last three digits Tristan's body cam had caught on the third van. Mud obscured the rest of the number plate.

'Run that past Ethiopian Road Transport Authority,' she instructed Pippa. 'And check the vehicle licensing agencies in Kenya, Somalia, South Africa, Zimbabwe, Namibia, and Botswana.'

'The Afrikaans link?' said Jason.

Rachel nodded. 'And where the cartel's been known to operate.'

Will shifted in his chair. 'Do you mind going back another twenty seconds on the clip? And slow the speed by thirty percent.'

They all looked at the former SEAL.

He shrugged. 'Humor me.'

Zac opened some video software and dropped the file in. A slow-motion version of the recording soon played across the screen.

'Stop.' Will narrowed his eyes. 'Rewind it eight seconds and drop the speed by fifty.'

Rachel frowned at the gritty images jumping across the monitor. She was looking for what the former SEAL had spotted.

'There!' said Will. 'Freeze it.'

Zac tapped a key.

'Zoom in on your nine o'clock.'

He focused the image.

'Shit,' said Lea. 'I see it.'

'Son of a bitch,' muttered Edison. He glanced at Will in admiration.

Rachel stared at the frozen still on the screen, heart pounding in her chest.

As the lead van pulled away, the camera had captured a reflection in the side mirror. It was the face of an unmasked man sitting in the front passenger seat.

❄

It was ten o'clock by the time they got a lucky break.

'Okay, here we go,' said Pippa. She opened a file and brought it up on the screen. A picture appeared on the left. To the right came a stream of data on the man they had identified from Tristan's body camera. 'Ulrich Armand Voigt. Ex-South African Special Forces. Awarded a Golden Leopard, South Africa's highest military decoration for bravery, for saving his men while under heavy enemy fire in the war in Angola in the 1990s. Retired in 2000. Started working for a private military contractor in Sierra Leone in 2005. Has been suspected of involvement in various coups across the African continent since then. There are also indications he may have links with terrorist groups in the Middle East.'

Jason scrutinized the man on the screen. Pippa had used a sophisticated piece of software to convert the infrared shot from Tristan's body camera into a visible spectrum image they could input into the U.S. government's Terrorist Identities Datamart, the FBI's National Crime Information Center, and Interpol's database of known and suspected criminals and terrorists. The probability that Voigt was their man was over ninety percent.

The mercenary had a hard face and eyes that spoke of years of experience on the battlefield. His Special Forces file showed extensive skills across all terrains and engagement in conflicts in some of the most dangerous places on Earth.

Jason frowned. *He won't be easy to bring down.*

'You think he's the leader of the cartel?' said Huck.

Rachel shook her head.

'I doubt it. The people at the top don't usually like to get their hands dirty.'

'He's probably training their men,' said Jason.

Rachel dipped her chin. 'I think so too.'

Jason's gaze shifted to the screen. In the last couple of hours, he had come to an embarrassing conclusion. He was seriously attracted to the woman now in charge of his team.

It was not her looks making him think some very unprofessional thoughts about her, although the whole tall, blonde, grey-eyed action chick thing would get any man's blood shifting south faster than you could yell morning glory.

Behind the veneer of confidence and strength she projected, he sensed a fragility that was seemingly invisible to everyone else in the room. The woman across from him had been hurt, badly at that. Yet, here she was, the leader of one of the best special ops teams in the world.

It made him want to know her better.

Still, you're a dick for thinking about this shit now.

His mood sobered at the thought of his best friend and the Vice President's daughter.

'Do we have any information about Voigt's last known whereabouts?' he said.

Pippa scrolled down the screen and opened another file. 'He was spotted in Mogadishu a month ago. Somalian National Intelligence got intel he was in town. They were tracking him but lost his trace somewhere near Bakaara market.'

Rachel stirred. 'What was he doing there?'

'They think he was meeting someone.'

'They have any idea who? Was it someone from the cartel?'

Before Pippa could reply, a video call appeared on the monitor. Jason stiffened. He recognized the number.

A window blinked open on the screen. Alex came into view. He was in tactical gear. Apprehension coursed through Jason. Alex was not alone. Alastair Caldwell stood beside him.

'We have news,' said Alex. 'A video was sent to the

Vice President's private email address thirty minutes ago.'

Jason's heart plummeted as he studied the men who had brought him into Division Eight.

'How bad is it?'

Caldwell's expression hardened.

'It's bad.'

❄

CHAPTER TWELVE

Two masked men pinned Melissa Hunt to the mattress of a camp bed. A third man stood above her, a leather whip in hand. Her cries echoed from the speakers as it struck the bare flesh of her back repeatedly. Blood ran in small rivulets from the welts on her skin and stained the sweat-soaked sheet beneath her.

A muffled grunt sounded from the left. The camera swung around. Tristan came into view. He was lying on the floor, arms tied behind his back, his face battered and bloodied. A masked man was applying a taser to his chest. Convulsions shook the former Ranger's body. His spine arched off the floor, tendons cording in his neck as his eyes rolled back into his head. They had placed a stick in his mouth to stop him from biting his tongue. From the burns on his T-shirt, his captors had been torturing him for some time.

The video lasted ten minutes and thirty seconds. A masked man stepped into the camera's viewfinder at the end, a sobbing Melissa and an unconscious Tristan in the background.

'This is a taste of things to come. We know about your special ops teams. If we see them, if we even smell them within a mile of us, we'll make him watch while we rape her, put a bullet through their heads, and post the whole thing on the Internet.'

Rachel stared at the static filling the feed, nails digging into her palms. Across the table, rage and agony were reflected in Jason's eyes in equal measure.

'Unforgivable,' said Lea, her tone echoing the palpable outrage in the room.

'They know about Division Eight,' said Caldwell. His voice was ice cold. 'We don't know how. Yet.'

Silence filled the room as they considered the implication of his words.

'Is everyone else thinking what I'm thinking?' said Claire stiffly. 'That this looks like an inside job?'

Clint nodded. 'I agree. The fact that they got to her so fast, the ambush in the Harenna Forest, and now this? It can't be a coincidence.'

Alex exchanged a glance with Caldwell. 'We're looking into it.'

'Who here believes this is about money?' said Lea.

Rachel studied the former CIA agent. Lea's instincts were rarely wrong.

'Why do you say that?'

'The ransom demand came more than twenty-four hours after Melissa's abduction. That right there is unusual.'

'She's correct,' Claire murmured.

'You think this is about political or ideological beliefs?' said Rachel.

Lea hesitated before shaking her head. 'No. If they wanted to hurt the United States, there are better ways of doing it. Ways that would attract worldwide media attention to their cause.'

'Bombs?' said Jason.

'Yes. I'm thinking U.S. embassies and hotels popular with American tourists. They could have their pick of targets on the northern African subcontinent.'

'What then?' said Alex.

A frustrated sigh left Lea's lips. 'I don't know.'

They updated Alex and Caldwell with the latest intel on Voigt before ending the video call.

Rachel glanced at her watch. They had under twenty hours left until the deadline.

She scanned the room. 'Here's what we should do.'

※

Tristan blinked his eyes open. Pain hit him with the force of a fourteen wheeler. He gasped and clenched his jaw, suddenly wishing for the numbness that had come with unconsciousness. He was lying on his side, face to the wall. He rolled over slowly. Bolts of lightning stabbed through his body from the muscles that had clenched uncontrollably during his repeated electrocution.

Relief darted through him when he saw the figure on the camp bed. 'Melissa?'

She raised her head off the pillow and turned to

look at him. Even that simple movement caused her to wince. Tristan's heart twisted as he studied her swollen, red eyes. They had dressed the wounds on her back and left her skin exposed to the air.

'You okay?' he murmured.

She nodded tremulously. 'You?'

He attempted a smile and regretted it straight away. 'I could be better.'

Melissa lowered her head to the bed, her eyes still on him. 'You were out for a while. I thought they'd killed you.'

Behind the concern and fear in her voice, Tristan detected a trace of anger. It pleased him. The moment she gave up was the moment her abductors would win the deadly game at hand.

'Do you think—' she swallowed and closed her eyes briefly, 'do you think my father's seen the video?'

Tristan hesitated. There was no point lying to her. 'Probably.'

She swore. He raised an eyebrow.

'What?'

'Nothing,' he muttered. 'Just—I was expecting more lady-like language.'

She stared. 'You do realize this is the twenty-first century, right?'

Tristan shrugged.

Melissa sighed. Silence fell between them.

'You probably think I'm some spoilt brat playing around pretending to be charitable, don't you?' she said after a while.

Tristan rolled onto his back and stared at the ceiling. 'I never said that.'

More silence followed.

'I love my father,' she said finally. 'I love my family. I couldn't have wished for a better upbringing. But I never asked to be born in the lap of luxury.' A trace of bitterness underscored her words. 'I wanted to give back. To make a difference to this world, not just through my father's name but with my own hands.' Her breath hitched in her throat. 'I never meant for people to die protecting me.'

Tristan's heart ached as he listened to her low sobs. 'What I do. What your bodyguards did. It's not a job. It's a vocation. We do it because we love our country. We do it to defend and protect the interests of its citizens. There is no better way to go than to die knowing we made a difference.' He turned his head and stared at her. 'Look at me.' He paused. *'Look at me.'*

Melissa finally opened her eyes.

'You are not at fault for what happened. You have to believe that.'

She hesitated before dipping her chin.

'Tristan?' she said after some time.

'Yeah?'

'I don't want to die.'

'Yeah.'

'I haven't even had sex yet.'

Tristan choked on his breath and gasped as pain shot through his abdomen.

She grimaced. 'Too much information?'

'Kinda.'

CHAPTER THIRTEEN

Their helicopter landed at Aden Adde airport in Mogadishu at thirteen hundred hours. Four Somalian National Intelligence agents were waiting for them when they exited the aircraft.

'You couldn't have come at a better time,' said the lead officer as they rode into the city. 'One of Voigt's men just resurfaced. A police officer spotted him in town forty minutes ago. I have an agent tailing him. We're on our way there now.'

Rachel could not stop the cold smile that curved her lips. Mogadishu had been the right call after all.

Following Alex and Caldwell's video call, she had asked the local Ethiopian army commander assisting them for the fastest way to get the Division Eight teams to the Somalian capital. The guy had grinned before indicating the hulking shape of a Mil Mi-24 Russian helicopter parked on the tarmac some five hundred feet away.

All that Somalian National Intelligence knew of

their mission was that they were after the East African drug cartel behind the deaths of three American citizens on the *Nostradamus*.

Twenty minutes after they touched down, they were in a temporary mobile command post in the back of a van two miles north of the airport.

'Huck, suspect is at your one o'clock,' said Rachel. She scanned the camera feeds displayed across Zac's laptop. 'Barry, he's at your eleven.'

'I see him,' Huck said quietly into his transmitter.

The former Marines had changed into plain clothes provided by the Somalian agents and were working their way up a busy avenue toward the Somalian operative shadowing Voigt's associate.

'Fuaad, fall back,' ordered the Somalian lead officer next to Rachel. 'You're too close.'

'Copy that,' said the Somalian agent.

The camera in Huck's sunglasses caught the operative subtly slowing his steps on the left. Twenty feet ahead of them, a man in jeans and a white shirt strolled along the pavement, a backpack on his shoulder.

'Remember guys, right now this is a simple recon mission,' said Jason on the other side of Rachel. 'Just see where he goes and what he does.'

The man they were tracking was one Abu Anwar Osman, a known criminal with suspected affiliations with the East African drug cartel Voigt was linked with. He was also one of the men who had been with the mercenary a month back, when Somalian intelligence officers lost their trace in the middle of the city.

'He's going into a computer repair shop,' said Barry a moment later. 'Maybe that's what he has in the bag. A laptop.'

Will's voice came over the communication link. 'There's a games store twenty feet ahead, on your right. Huck and Fuaad, you've got the coffee shop across the road.'

The former SEAL was on the roof of a building two hundred feet west of the van. His scope cam gave them a straight-line view down the avenue where Fuaad had tracked Osman.

Three hundred feet east, at a major intersection the suspect would have to pass if he carried on down the road, Edison's scope cam showed them the diametrically opposite perspective.

'Think the shop's a front?' said Jessica.

'I don't think so,' said the Somalian lead agent. 'None of our intel suggests a connection with the cartel.'

Jason turned to Rachel. This close, she could see the gunmetal grey specks in his eyes and feel the heat from his body. It sent tingles down her spine.

'What do you want to do?' he said.

'He's coming out of the building. The bag's gone,' said Huck.

Rachel's gaze shifted to the video feeds. She could no longer deny her growing attraction to Jason Scott. Fortunately, she didn't have time to linger on that startling realization.

'Fuaad, Huck, keep tailing him. Barry, go in and see if you can spot the bag.'

The view from Barry's button camera darkened as he entered the shop. He walked over to a display cabinet filled with second-hand mobile phones and perused its contents. Someone called out to him.

The former Marine turned and headed for the counter where a shop assistant stood, a smile on his face.

'Hi there,' said Barry. 'I'm looking for a charger for an iPhone 5s.'

The shop assistant nodded and bent to rummage in the glass case beneath the counter.

'On the shelf to the left,' said Jason.

Barry shifted slightly. The bag Osman had walked into the shop with came into focus amidst a collection of other electronic devices.

Rachel turned to the Somalian lead agent. 'We need that bag.'

He dialed a number as Barry completed his purchase and headed back to the mobile command post. Moments later, a Somalian patrol car parked at the curb in front of the store. Two officers got out and went inside. They returned to their vehicle within minutes, an evidence bag in hand. The patrol car pulled out into the avenue and headed slowly in their direction.

The Somalian agent opened the side door of the van and grabbed the evidence bag one of the officers passed to him through a window.

'Huck, Fuaad, where are you?' said Rachel.

She watched as Jason slipped some gloves on and carefully extracted the backpack from the evidence carrier. There was a laptop inside.

Huck's voice came over the communication line. 'We're at a commercial center. He's browsing an electronics shop, looking at new computers.'

'Keep tailing him. Let's see where he ends up.'

'Will do.'

It was another half hour before Osman finally got off the streets.

'He just entered an apartment complex,' said Huck. 'Seems he's intending to stay a while. He picked up take out on the way here.'

'Can you tell where he is?' said Rachel.

She steadied herself against the roof and wall of the van as she studied the white and ochre eight-story structure visible on Huck's camera feed. They were on the move to the address, in a suburb north of the city.

'Not without walking inside and knocking on doors,' said Fuaad. 'We'd be going in blind.'

The Somalian operative had completed a perimeter check of the area. A small grocery store stood to the left of the building. Beyond a fence to the right was a residential quarter of one and two-story houses. A fire escape ran down the north wall of the apartment complex from the rooftop to a side alley next to the fence. The car park at the rear backed onto a deserted street and an abandoned construction site for another apartment building.

'Okay, here it is,' said Zac.

Somalian Intelligence had pulled a list of the

occupants of the building from the city's tax and poll registers and forwarded it to his computer.

'There,' said the Somalian lead agent. He pointed at a name halfway down the listing. 'That's one of Osman's aliases. He's in Apartment 6B.'

'How long before we can see floor plans of that building?' said Jason.

The Somalian agent rubbed his chin thoughtfully. 'Thirty minutes, forty tops.'

Tension coursed through Rachel. They were running out of time.

'We need to go in there,' she said. 'Get us those plans.'

The Somalian agent took out his cell and spoke to one of his operatives. Moments later, their van pulled in at the curb some two hundred feet south of the building.

'Will, I want you high up on that construction block at the back,' said Rachel. 'Edison, take the water tower on the street we just passed. You should get a good view of anything happening at the front.'

The two snipers exited the vehicle.

※

It was fifteen hundred hours when Somalian intelligence finally sent them scanned schematics of the building.

'Jason, Claire, you go in through the front,' said Rachel. Her finger moved across the floor plan. 'Huck and Jessica, take the rear. Barry and Fuaad, you guard the exits on the ground. It seems the fire escape is only accessible from the rooftop and a fire door on each floor, so it should be safe. Remember, there are civilians inside that building so keep live fire to a minimum. Will and Edison will be keeping an eye out on the front and back access.'

Jason straightened from the table. 'We should ask local police to set up a perimeter.'

Rachel studied him with a faint smile; it was what she had been about to request. 'Agreed.' She turned to the Somalian lead agent. 'We'll go in once you give us the all-clear.'

❋

JASON CROUCHED NEAR THE NORTH END OF THE SIXTH floor corridor, his Beretta M9 in hand and Claire at his side. Huck and Jessica stood with their backs against the wall fifteen feet to the left, on the other side of apartment 6B.

Rachel's voice came over the transmitter in Jason's ear. 'Everyone in position?'

He was about to respond when a door opened opposite him. An elderly lady in a bright floral dress appeared in the doorway of 6A, a walking cane in one hand and a shopping bag in the other.

'Hang on a second,' Jason murmured.

He smiled at the old woman, pressed a finger to his lips, and shook his head. She stared at him for a shocked moment, peeked at Claire, Huck, and Jessica, and shuffled hastily back inside the apartment. The door slammed shut.

'We're going in,' said Jason.

He signaled to the others and moved to the door of apartment 6B. They flanked him as he rose and aimed his gun at the lock. He fired twice and kicked the door in with Huck's help.

They went in low, arms moving around in one hundred eighty arcs as they swept the minimally furnished, open plan living and kitchen area.

There was no sign of Osman.

Jason glanced at the plate of half-eaten food and empty bottle of Coke on the table before moving to the archway on the right, the others on his heels. He paused when he reached the opening. There was a passage to the left. Two doors stood further along it. They were both closed.

He motioned to Jessica and Claire, his pulse thrumming in his veins. They headed for the first door while he and Huck carried on down the passage to the far one.

They went in on his signal. A small, empty bathroom opened up on the other side of the second door.

Just as Jessica shouted, 'Clear!' from the next room, Jason's gaze alighted on the narrow opening high above the toilet. 'Shit! He's gone out through the window.'

He climbed on top of the cistern and scaled the wall, Huck behind him.

'Will, Edison, is he in your sight?' Rachel barked over the comm line.

'That's a negative,' said Will.

'Same here,' said Edison. 'He's in my blind spot.'

Hot air washed over Jason when he squeezed through the window. He looked out and saw Osman on the fire escape ten feet to the right. Something caught his gaze. There was a rope dangling from a waste pipe within arm's reach of the bathroom window.

Jason scowled. *Bastard planned his exit route ages ago. That rope's invisible from the ground.*

'Rachel, he's on the fire escape to the north!' he snapped into his transmitter.

He grabbed the rope and used gravity to swing across to the metal platform.

'How the hell did he—?' started Rachel.

'The clever son of a bitch had his escape route all figured out!'

Jason started rapidly down the stairs, Huck seconds behind him.

Twenty feet below, Osman dashed down the fire escape two steps at a time, shirt flapping wildly in the wind as he raced for the ground. Metal juddered beneath Jason and Huck as they gave chase.

Osman suddenly stopped and looked up. Sunlight glinted on the barrel of the weapon in his hand. Jason swore and grabbed Huck.

Bullets whizzed past them as they flattened themselves against the side of the building. One of Osman's shots struck the metal platform two feet from Huck's boots.

The Marine leaned over the handrail and returned fire. 'Go! I'll cover you!'

Jason nodded and headed down. Osman turned and resumed his desperate escape. A figure appeared at the north end of the alley just as he reached the first floor landing. It was Fuaad.

Osman raised his gun and shot at the Somalian agent. The latter dove into the shelter of a nearby dumpster and returned fire.

Jason glanced at the crowded houses beyond the fence. *We can't let him make it into that residential area!*

Barry came into view at the south end of the alley. Osman stumbled toward the ground, his shots wild and desperate as he fired at the two agents flanking him.

The diversion bought Jason the precious seconds he needed. He climbed onto the handrail of the fire escape and jumped just as Osman started for the fence.

The man turned at the last moment, eyes flaring in surprise and gun swinging around. Then Jason was on top of him.

❄

CHAPTER FOURTEEN

'There are three potential addresses for the partial plate from the van in the Harenna Forest.' Pippa's voice came over the phone link on Zac's computer. 'Bosaso, in the Bari province of Somalia. Haranka, in Middle Juba. And Meru, in Eastern Kenya.'

Rachel marked the locations on the map on the wall. 'Okay, thanks.'

They were in a safe house owned by Somalian National Intelligence, on the outskirts of Mogadishu. Osman's laptop and mobile phone sat on the table in the middle of the room. Muffled thuds traveled through the ceiling from where he was being interrogated upstairs.

Lea came on the line. 'How are things at your end?'

'We hit the jackpot. One of the men who was in the city with Voigt last month happened to be in town. Somalian National Intelligence helped us capture him. Zac is analyzing his computer right now.'

'Has he talked?' said Lea.

Something heavy landed on the floor above.

'No,' said Rachel. 'But I suspect he will soon.'

'I've got some news.'

Rachel straightened at Lea's tone. *It's good I let her stay back in Addis Ababa with Pippa and Clint.*

'I've been looking at CCTV recordings from buildings and public places within a mile of Bakaara market, from the day Voigt and his men were last spotted in Mogadishu. I reckoned he might have set up the meet somewhere close by.'

'What did you find?'

'He spent twenty minutes talking to a guy in a hotel about a thousand feet from where Somalian National Intelligence lost his trace.'

A thrill shot through Rachel. 'You got a face?'

'No. The cameras in the hotel lobby and outside the room where they met only caught the guy's figure. He was wearing a Panama hat. Definitely Caucasian. Looked middle-aged.'

'How did he get to and from the hotel?'

'Chauffeur-driven sedan from a local car hire place,' said Clint on the phone line. 'The hotel room and the car were booked under a fake passport.'

Rachel could tell from his clipped voice that he had not completely forgiven her for ordering him to stay in Ethiopia. 'Can you send us the video?'

'Will do,' said Clint. He ended the call.

The door opened. Jason walked in with Barry and the lead Somalian intelligence officer.

'He's a tough son of a bitch,' said Jason in response to her silent stare. He rubbed his red knuckles.

The Somalian agent grimaced. 'Osman says the cartel has his sister. If he talks, they'll kill her.'

Rachel narrowed her eyes. 'You believe him?'

The agent hesitated. 'That's often the way with these gangs. Osman is a clever man. If there was a way out of it, he would have done something by now.'

Her heart sank. *Shit. He's not going to talk.* She looked at the clock on the wall. *And we're almost out of time.*

'You got anything from Osman's computer?' Jason asked Zac.

'He wasn't lying when he said it was broken. Hard drive is fried. I've recovered a handful of files. Just loading them up to our servers now.'

'Bring up the CCTV recording first,' said Rachel.

Jason frowned. 'What CCTV recording?'

Rachel updated them with EAGLE's latest findings. A minute later, the video Pippa had transferred across played on Zac's computer screen. They watched it from the moment the figure in the white suit and Panama hat entered the hotel to when he exited it with Voigt a half hour later.

Jason frowned at the frozen still of the white man in the hat shaking hands with the mercenary. 'That guy is an American.'

They turned and stared at him.

Rachel was unable to mask the surprise in her voice. 'You know him?'

Jason hesitated. 'I think so. The way he carries himself.' His expression hardened. 'I've seen him before.'

Rachel studied the image on the screen, her mind racing. 'You have any idea when?'

He ran a hand through his hair, his eyes dark with frustration. 'Sometime in the last two years, I think.'

She turned to the Somalian agent. 'You got a dry erase board?'

※

'Here's what we know so far about Melissa Hunt's abduction.'

Jason scrutinized the mind map Rachel had drawn on the wall. WOLF and EAGLE were the only ones in the room. She had asked the Somalian intelligence agent to step out for a moment.

'There was no intel about a possible threat to her person. We suspect this was an inside job and that the ransom demand is a front for something else. Whoever is feeding information to the group behind the kidnapping knows about Division Eight. They knew of the rescue mission in Harenna. The man from the hotel may be that informant.' She paused. 'What's the connection?'

'Washington,' said Jessica.

Rachel turned to her. 'Why do you say that?'

'It's the obvious thing that links the Vice President and Division Eight.'

Rachel smiled faintly. 'I agree. The fact that Jason may have met this guy in the last two years also points to D.C.'

Admiration darted through him. Rachel had come to that conclusion faster than anyone in the room.

'It's unlikely to be anyone in the teams,' he said.

Rachel nodded. 'So someone with inside knowledge of Division Eight and access to its operations. I think we can safely rule out Alastair Caldwell and the President. That leaves us with members of Congress.'

'That's a pretty bold assumption we're making,' said Claire.

Rachel studied her for a moment. 'Do you think we're on the wrong track?'

'No, I'm pretty certain you're right.' The WOLF team member sighed. 'I'm just saying we're gonna ruffle a lot of feathers on Capitol Hill once we put this out there.'

'No one else has to know apart from Alex and Caldwell right now.' Rachel's face hardened. 'Besides, if this saves Tristan and Melissa, I'm happy to face whatever consequences come my way.' She glanced at Jason. 'It's my decision as team leader.'

A fresh wave of respect washed over Jason. Rachel Carter was someone he was definitely going to get to know better once this mission was over. He looked around the room and saw the fresh conviction her words inspired in everyone's expressions.

'They're pretty much gonna have to go after all of us if that's the case,' he said with a smile.

'Yep,' muttered Jessica.

The others nodded.

'So, how do we do this?' said Huck.

Rachel frowned. 'I want Pippa, Clint, and Lea to

work the D.C. angle with Alex. It will buy us time while we try to squeeze any intel we can get out of Osman.'

'I know something that will drastically reduce Pippa and the others' workload,' said Zac. He grinned in the face of their stares. 'GAIT technology. They can use it to analyze videos of the Congress members. See if it matches our mystery man with any of them.'

Rachel nodded briskly. 'Get Pippa and Lea on it. I want you to look at the files from Osman's computer.'

※

'This was taken at the harbor in Bosaso two weeks ago,' said Zac.

The first tendrils of unease coiled through Rachel.

They were studying one of the pictures he had pulled from Osman's phone. Luckily for them, the guy had not erased the metadata on the JPEG file. It had allowed Zac to identify the date, time, and location where the shot had been taken.

The image showed a view from the stern of a ship. Sunlight danced on the blue-green waters of the port in the background. Fishing vessels and freighters dotted the ocean in the distance.

Rachel wrote down the Bosaso address Pippa had identified on a notepad, ripped the page out, and walked over to the door.

'Can you get local police to check this place out?' She handed the note to the Somalian intelligence agent waiting outside. 'It's important we get someone from your team there ASAP.'

The agent studied her for a moment before taking the sheet. 'Sure.' He slipped his cell phone out of his pocket and hesitated, finger hovering above the screen. His dark gaze focused on her face. 'I have a feeling you're not telling me the whole truth, Agent Carter.'

Rachel clamped down on the nervous tension running through her limbs. 'I'm not. And it has to stay that way unless I'm told otherwise by my superiors.'

The Somalian agent frowned.

'Okay,' he said finally. 'As long as you don't get any of my agents killed, I can live with that.'

Rachel nodded and closed the door.

'You think the ship's got anything to do with this?' said Jessica.

'I hope not,' Rachel muttered.

Jessica raised an eyebrow.

'I don't like ships.'

❋

It was an hour before Somalian Intelligence got back to them.

'The van was registered to a warehouse a mile from the harbor.' The Somalian lead agent's eyes blazed with satisfaction as he spoke. 'I had two agents close by investigating another case. Luckily for Bosaso police, they were there when they entered the premises. There was a gunfight with members of the cartel. They injured one man and arrested another two. They found five hundred pounds of cocaine stashed inside mini excavators bound for Turkey.' He smiled. 'They also found an order for provisions delivered to a ship docked there two weeks ago. The vessel's name is the *MV Bonneville*.'

A buzzing noise filled Rachel's ears. She caught the quizzical look Jason gave her and suppressed the panic threatening to swallow her.

'Look it up,' she instructed Zac.

It was several minutes before he found the ship's details in a maritime database. 'The *Bonneville* is a class 3 chemical tanker of Japanese origin. It was sold by Tokyo Marine to a specialist chemical company in Yemen three years ago.'

'We have details of the company?' said Jason.

'Pulling up the files right now.'

The clatter of the keyboard was loud in the strained silence.

'Hmm,' Zac murmured.

'What?' said Rachel.

'This company may very well be a front for our drug cartel. I'm seeing bank accounts and subsidiaries all over the place.'

Rachel fought down a wave of nausea. 'Send the details to Division Eight and the DEA,' she ordered stiffly.

Jason glanced at her with a faint frown before turning to Zac. 'Can you find out the *Bonneville*'s current location?'

'I should be able to if their Automatic Identification System is still active.' Zac brought up a couple of live vessel tracking sites and entered the name of the tanker. 'Well, that's interesting. Looks like their AIS went dark twenty hours ago. Last radar contact placed the ship twenty-five miles north west of Bosaso, in the Gulf of Aden.'

Dark spots filled Rachel's vision. The buzzing in her ears intensified.

'See if we can get eyes on that ship,' she said between numb lips. 'Ask the NGA for geo-spatial intelligence for the Gulf of Aden from the time WOLF's mission ended yesterday. And get Caldwell to authorize a UAV from the closest U.S. military base or aircraft carrier. I'll be back in a moment.'

Willing her legs not to collapse beneath her, Rachel rose to her feet and headed for the exit. There was an empty washroom at the back of the house. She knelt in front of the toilet and threw up in the bowl.

She was standing at the sink splashing cold water on her face when the door opened. Jason stepped in. He studied her pale face before closing the door and leaning against it.

'What's going on?' he said quietly.

Rachel's gaze shifted to the cracked mirror above the sink. She avoided the haunted expression clouding her eyes and splashed more water on her face.

Jason waited silently, his pose that of a man with all the time in the world.

She turned off the faucet and leaned on the sink, head bowed as she fought the storm of emotions drowning her. Even though they had yet to confirm whether Tristan and Melissa were on the *Bonneville*, everything inside her was screaming that that was exactly where they were. The ship was the perfect place for hostages. It offered little chance of escape and would be a nightmare for anyone planning a rescue mission.

And it was what she would do if she were in Voigt's shoes.

She clenched her fists. *Damn it, Carter! This is not the Nostradamus and you are not that woman anymore.*

'Rachel?' Jason prompted, concern underscoring his voice.

She stared at his reflection in the mirror. *He deserves to know.*

❄

CHAPTER FIFTEEN

Jason resisted the urge to cross the room and take Rachel in his arms. The tormented expression on her face was one he had never seen before and it made him ache. Still, he forced himself to stay still and waited for her to talk.

'How much do you know about the DEA's FAST teams?' she said hesitantly.

Surprise darted through him. 'I know enough.'

She took a deep breath. 'Two years ago, I became a member of a FAST team led by Benjamin Westfield, a senior DEA agent. We were based in Afghanistan, where Vivian Thorpe trained me. Benjamin and I—' She paused and bit her lip. 'Benjamin and I became lovers six months later. We couldn't carry on working together so I requested a transfer back to Quantico. I was still in Afghanistan when we were assigned the mission to rescue the hostages aboard the *Nostradamus*.'

Remorse stabbed through Jason as he recalled details of the incident aboard the vessel; he hadn't known she was part of *that* DEA team. Acid filled his stomach. He knew what was coming next.

'The pirates' ringleader had rigged a bomb on the bridge.' Her voice remained cold and clinical. 'There was no indication he was intending to blow up the vessel. I was behind Benjamin when it detonated.' Her breath hitched in her throat. She closed her eyes and swallowed convulsively. 'No. More like, Benjamin stepped in front of me when he realized what was going to happen.'

Jason's heart pounded in his chest at her words.

'I was the only one on the bridge who survived the explosion. Benjamin's body protected me from the brunt of it.' She crossed her arms protectively across her body. 'We—we got engaged a week earlier.'

Jason listened wordlessly as she spoke of the aftermath of the *Nostradamus* incident and her faltering career at the DEA.

'Vivian found me eight months later and recruited me into Division Eight. The rest is history.'

She lapsed into silence, a dull expression on her face. Once more, Jason fought the irrational urge to take her in his arms. Despite the pain etched deep in her grey eyes, he knew she would object to the action.

'We don't know they're on that ship.'

A mocking smile twisted her lips. 'You and I both know that's horseshit.'

He watched her for a moment before sighing. She was right. 'It's what Voigt would do.'

'Yes.' She rubbed the back of her neck and seemed

to come to a decision. 'I think you should lead the mission from now on.'

Jason blinked, unsure he'd heard her right.

'I'll call Alex and let him know. We can tell—'

'No,' he said vehemently.

She stopped and studied him for a beat. 'I may not be able to—'

'So we co-lead,' said Jason. 'If I see you slipping up, I take over.'

She was quiet for some time. 'These are your people.'

'And I trust you to lead them,' said Jason.

Even as the words left his lips, the former Ranger knew he meant every single one.

Rachel grimaced and ran a hand through her hair. 'Anyone ever tell you you're a stubborn ass?'

'My mother and my three sisters,' said Jason. 'Practically every single day while I was still at home and every time I've visited since then.'

A faint smile curved her lips. His gaze dropped to her mouth. A different urge filled him then, a slow heat that promised to turn into an inferno.

Her expression sobered, as if she'd read his mind. 'Let's head back.'

She walked past him and exited the room. Jason silently cursed his untimely libido and followed in her footsteps. They got several quizzical stares when they returned to the makeshift command room. Jason blanked them out and glanced at Rachel.

Fully composed, she turned to Zac. 'What's the status on that UAV?'

It was the *Nostradamus* mission all over again, with a couple of unexpected twists.

The incongruity of their current situation was not lost on Rachel as she studied the thermal infrared images displayed on one of the computer consoles inside the Combat Information Center of the U.S. Navy warship currently speeding though the waters of the Gulf of Aden on an interception course with the *Bonneville*.

It was gone two in the morning. Nearly seven hours had passed since the NGA had identified the location of the chemical tanker sixty miles north west of Bosaso from their satellite imagery. It was another forty minutes before the MQ-9 Reaper UAV launched from Camp Lemonnier, the U.S. Africa Command base in Djibouti, confirmed what Rachel had suspected. The *Bonneville* was housing an inordinate number of armed men considering its cargo holds were meant to be empty. Thermal infrared imaging the drone transmitted live from the vessel's position also showed two possible prisoners in the superstructure on the ship's main deck.

Lea had flown in from Addis Ababa by the time they landed on the *USS Harrogate*. The amphibious transport dock warship had been on a training exercise in the Gulf of Aden and was reassigned to their mission by the U.S. Secretary of Defense. Pippa and Clint remained in Ethiopia, working the Washington angle and overseeing the rescue mission with Zac.

Captain Taylor, the commander of the *USS Harrogate*, turned to Rachel. 'We're fifty miles north of the Somalian coastline. We should be in position in the next fifteen minutes.'

She nodded and headed for the well deck of the warship, where the Navy SEAL platoon standing by to assist WOLF and EAGLE if things went south were helping them get ready.

With less than four hours left until the deadline set by Voigt and the drug cartel, Rachel knew that if the rescue mission currently in play proved unsuccessful, Tristan and Melissa would be dead before sunrise.

And not just them.

A fresh wave of anxiety coursed through her as she slipped into a drysuit and glanced at the men and women who were about to put their lives in her hands. She clamped down on her dark thoughts and repeated the mantra she had been telling herself for the last few hours.

This is different. You're different. And you have two of the best black ops teams in the world working with you on this.

Ten minutes later, WOLF and EAGLE were in full combat diving gear. Rachel gave her weapons the once over and examined the magazines in the waterproof utility belt at her waist. A Navy SEAL did the final check on her MK 25 and the closed circuit SCUBA rebreathers her team would be using to get to their target.

'Okay,' he said. 'You're ready.'

Rachel nodded her thanks and turned to face

WOLF and EAGLE. Jason watched her silently, his blue eyes calm and full of encouragement. The others looked just as relaxed, despite the adrenaline she had no doubt was buzzing through their veins.

Her resolve hardened in the face of their unreserved trust. *You better not sink, Carter.*

'Let's go.'

They moved to the torpedo-shaped crafts sitting in the flooded wet well in the stern of the warship.

There's twist number one, Rachel thought wryly.

Unlike the diver propulsion scooters the FAST team had utilized to board the *Nostradamus*, WOLF and EAGLE would be using two Mark 8 Mod 1 SEAL Delivery Vehicles, free-flooding wet submersibles deployed by the SEALs during covert ops, to get to their target.

Will and Dustin took the pilot seats of the two SDVs; as former SEALs, they had already been trained on using the crafts. Rachel stepped inside the copilot chair of the first submersible while Jason slipped in the one aboard the second vehicle. The rest of WOLF and EAGLE held on to the hand and foot grips on the fuselages.

Rachel placed her mouthpiece gently between her teeth, opened her regulator, and pulled down her diving mask. She checked the crew on her SDV, got a thumbs up from Jason, and signaled to Will and Dustin. Thirty seconds later, they were in the water and headed for the *Bonneville*.

Once again, Rachel thanked the stroke of fate that had brought the *USS Harrogate* into their path. The stealth technology aboard the *San Antonio* class warship meant they were able to get within a few miles of the *Bonneville* without being detected. This was a pleasant change from the distance her FAST team had had to dive to get to the *Nostradamus*.

It took just half an hour before the bulbous bow of the chemical tanker appeared in the dark waters ahead. Jason's SDV veered off to the left and disappeared toward the vessel's stern. They would be boarding the ship from opposing directions.

Rachel helped Will put the submersible in hover mode below the ship while the others took off their SCUBA gear and kicked up silently to the surface of the ocean. They went up seconds later and emerged next to Barry bobbing in the water. His gaze was on the hull of the ship. Huck and Lea were already a third of the way up it.

Rachel stared. *And there's the second twist.*

Part of the training exercise the SEALs had been assigned on the *USS Harrogate* had been to test the effectiveness of the new Geckskin gloves and boot covers DARPA had designed for use by the U.S. Military. A synthetically-fabricated, reversible adhesive inspired by the gecko's ability to climb pretty much any surface in the world, the Geckskin could technically allow soldiers to stealthily scale vertical walls while carrying fifty pounds of combat gear. After two weeks of practice with a dozen of the prototypes, the SEALs had given them two thumbs up.

Barry swam for the starboard side of the ship.

Rachel and Will headed for the port side, latched on to the hull, and started climbing.

Halfway up, Rachel paused and spoke quietly into the sub assault headset under her dive hood. 'WOLF Six, this is EAGLE One. How are we looking, over?'

'EAGLE One, this is WOLF Six. There are five tangos on the forecastle deck, stand by, out,' Zac replied.

From his position on the *USS Harrogate*, he had a bird's eye view of the entire operation thanks to the thermal infrared feed from the MQ-9 Reaper still circling the *Bonneville* at high altitude.

'EAGLE Two, tango at your two o'clock, ten meters, over,' said Zac.

'Roger that WOLF Six, out,' murmured Lea over the comm line.

'EAGLE Three, tango at your eleven o'clock, fifteen meters, over,' said Zac.

Huck acknowledged the transmission.

Under Zac's direction, Rachel and Will climbed aboard the vessel and silently eliminated the other three armed guards patrolling the bow. They dragged the bodies of the dead men behind the anchor and mooring gear before joining Lea and Huck in the shadows of the pipe manifold running the length of the ship.

They found Barry next to a hose crane. He was wiping his bloodied knife on his drysuit, two dead men at his feet.

'EAGLE One, there are three tangos at your twelve

o'clock. Twenty meters out, three meters up. They're on the catwalk, out,' said Zac.

'Copy that, over,' said Rachel.

They moved swiftly alongside the pipes and halted beneath the metal platform running starboard to port. The guards stood evenly spaced out on the walkway, their eyes out to sea. Rachel signaled to the others.

Huck and Lea continued toward the dark shape rising from the main deck two hundred feet south of their position. Will and Barry headed left and right. Rachel climbed on top of a pipe below the middle of the platform, grabbed the metal edge, and pulled up smoothly behind one of the guards.

She slipped her Kbar out, clamped a hand over the man's mouth, and slit his throat in one smooth motion. He jerked in her embrace, his choked gurgles muffled by her fingers. She held him until he went limp and slowly lowered his body to the walkway.

The platform trembled as Will and Barry joined her. They slipped down between the manifold and made for a doorway at the base of the superstructure holding the ship's control rooms and crew quarters. The bridge was forty feet above them.

Rachel scanned the main deck, ears straining for any sounds that might indicate their infiltration had been spotted by the enemy. She heard nothing untoward.

'WOLF One, this is EAGLE One, what is your position, over?'

Jason's voice came over the comm line. 'EAGLE One, we're in the engine room. Ready to proceed, out.'

Adrenaline surged through her, hastening her heartbeat and sharpening her instincts. 'WOLF Six, what does the field look like, over?'

'EAGLE One, the deck is clear. EAGLE Two and EAGLE Three are in position above you,' said Zac. 'The mission is a go, out.'

Rachel took a shallow breath and slipped her Sig out of the waterproof pouch on her thigh. 'All stations, this is EAGLE One. On my mark in three, two, *one!*'

❄

CHAPTER SIXTEEN

TRISTAN FROZE AT THE DISTANT SOUND OF GUNFIRE.

A grim smile curved his lips. *About time!*

He glanced at the dark outline of the door before concentrating on the wooden stake in his hands, his heart thudding in his chest. Melissa knelt next to him, a stick gripped between her thighs; she was sharpening the end with the edge of a wire. They exchanged a glance.

It was thirty minutes since she had ripped open the mattress on a sharp edge of the camp bed and extracted the coiled spring Tristan had used to cut the ties binding his hands and feet.

With time running out and the deadline for the ransom only hours away, the former Ranger had seen no option but to attempt a desperate escape from the heart of the enemy's stronghold. When he told Melissa of his plans, she agreed without hesitation, raising his esteem for her once more. He broke two of the wooden supports in the bed and showed her how to use the coiled spring wire to turn them into stakes.

The bed now stood against the door, frame jammed beneath the handle. Though it wouldn't stop anyone from getting into the room, it would slow them down considerably.

An explosion went off somewhere in the ship. The floor shook beneath them. More gunfire broke out in the aftermath of the boom. Footsteps echoed outside the cell. Someone tried the door handle. It twisted a quarter of an inch before becoming stuck on the bed frame. The man outside cursed in Afrikaans and turned the handle frantically. The frame held. There was a thud as he rammed his shoulder against the door.

Tristan rose to his feet, took Melissa's hand, and guided her to the bulkhead behind the door. 'Remember, aim low. Go for the gut and the chest. No wild swings. And stay behind me.'

Melissa nodded shakily, her knuckles white on the shaft of the makeshift weapon. More thuds came from the door. Someone fired an assault rifle at close range. Bullets thudded into the escutcheon plate holding the lock and handle. The bed frame shifted.

Tristan rose on the balls on his feet and gripped the stake, adrenaline buzzing through his veins. The men outside kicked the door again. The bed frame shuddered and gave way in a screech of smashing wood. Light spilled into the room.

Tristan jammed the stake in the throat of the first man who came through the doorway, grabbed his assault rifle as he dropped the weapon, twisted the sling, and shot the second man in the chest. The latter stumbled against the far bulkhead before sliding to the floor, eyes wide and a trail of blood marking his body's path to the ground.

Tristan recovered the men's rifles and Beretta M9 pistols before inspecting the passage outside. The sounds of gunfights echoed from the lower decks. He grabbed Melissa's hand and headed left toward an intersection.

An armed man turned the corner when they were ten feet from the junction. Tristan shot him in the head, his stride unbroken. Melissa's breath warmed the back of his neck as he stopped and crouched at the corner of the bulkhead. He poked his head out. A bullet whizzed past his face from the left and slammed into the wall at the opposite end of the passage. He drew back sharply and caught Melissa's anxious look.

Tristan gave her an encouraging smile before slipping the stake and a Beretta out of his waistband. He lobbed the wooden stick across the intersection, lunged forward, and fired at the man discharging his assault rifle at the wrong spot. The guard went down. Another two appeared behind him.

Tristan swore and scrambled back into the cover of the passage, a storm of bullets raining down around him. Pulse thrumming rapidly, he scanned his surroundings for another escape route. There were none.

He rose to his feet and turned to Melissa. 'When I say go, I want you to run to the other end of that passage. Don't stop. Don't look back.'

She stared at him, hazel eyes brimming with tears. 'Okay.'

Tristan grabbed an assault rifle in each hand and was about to step out into the intersection when he felt a light grip his shoulder. Melissa rose on her toes and kissed him on the cheek. He blinked, surprised at the heat of her lips.

She nodded her readiness, her face grim with determination. Tristan dipped his chin, stepped out in the passage, and fired at the men at the other end with both rifles.

'Go!' he shouted over his shoulder.

He felt her move behind him and started running backward, smoke filling the corridor and the smell of gunpowder scorching the air. He headed after Melissa's disappearing figure.

❄

Air left Rachel's lungs in a whoosh as she ducked beneath a swinging blade. She struck the man holding the knife with a reverse roundhouse kick to the head, shot the guy behind him, and moved past their falling bodies.

The mission had been going to plan until five minutes ago, when someone spotted the empty catwalk where three guards should have been. WOLF had sabotaged the ship's engines, making it dead in the water, and had been working their way quietly up the aft of the superstructure while Rachel and her team proceeded at the opposite end.

By Zac's account, they had disposed of over half the men by the time the alarm was raised.

'EAGLE One, be advised our two birds are on the loose and making their way toward the ship's control room, out,' said Zac.

'They are *what?!*' Jason snapped on the comm line, all radio procedure out the window.

'Looks like Tristan got impatient playing Marian to your Robin Hood,' muttered Dustin.

Jason swore. 'He's going to get himself and Melissa killed.'

'No, he's not,' said Zac. 'He's already incapacitated five tangos. And I think Melissa Hunt just stabbed someone.'

Rachel exchanged surprised glances with Will and Barry. There was movement up ahead. She shot a man before he could raise his assault rifle and changed her magazine.

They were nearly at the control room.

※

Tristan's stomach dropped. He skidded to a halt just inside the doorway leading to the ship's bridge, heart suddenly racing with fear.

The blue-eyed mercenary with the shaved head was standing at the far end of the control room, a gun jammed against Melissa's temple. She stood frozen in her captor's grip, face pale and pupils dilated as she stared back at Tristan.

On their race through the ship, fighting the men on

their tail and seeking the team leading the rescue attempt, Melissa had stumbled straight into the enemy's hands.

'Put the guns down or I'll shoot her,' said the mercenary.

Shit. I should have kept her behind me.

Tristan cursed himself for his lack of foresight and slowly lowered the Beretta in his hands. The other men in the room rapidly divested him of his other weapons.

'On your knees,' the mercenary ordered.

Tristan hesitated before slowly lowering himself to the floor. The barrel of a pistol kissed the back of his head. He gazed unflinchingly at the man across the room.

'I have to say, your black ops team has balls.' The mercenary's eyes darkened with anger. 'The question is, are they stupid enough to get both of you killed? Because there is no question that I am going to execute one of you before they get here.'

He moved his hand and aimed the gun at Tristan, a savage smile twisting his face. 'Don't take this personally but I'm afraid the first one to die will have to be you. She is worth more to me alive than dead right now.'

Tristan read the despair in Melissa's expression. He gritted his teeth and saw the mercenary's finger shift to the trigger.

There are worse ways to die. I just wish I'd saved her first.

'Close your eyes,' he told Melissa softly.

The starboard bridge door slammed open. Three

armed figures in drysuits stepped inside, their weapons raised. Tristan's heart lurched in his chest when he recognized Jason, Claire, and Dustin.

'It's over, Voigt,' said Jason. 'Your men are dead and the *Bonneville* is currently in the line of sight of a U.S. warship. Put your guns down and release the hostages.'

The mercenary laughed wildly. 'You really think you have the upper hand? When I could snuff her life out with a single twitch of my finger?'

He tightened his hold on Melissa and forced the barrel of the gun into her temple once more. She winced, a tear running down her cheek.

❄

Rachel peered through the window of the control room.

Voigt stood at her two o'clock, a gun pointed at Melissa Hunt's temple. He had his back to the ship's consoles and the bay of windows overlooking the main deck.

Across the way from them, Tristan Payne was on his knees, a pistol at the back of his head. On the starboard side, at her twelve o'clock, Jason, Claire, and Dustin leveled their weapons at Voigt and the four armed men in the room. The scene bore all the hallmarks of a nasty Mexican stand off.

Gunfire sounded from the lower levels of the superstructure. Shouts and screams followed as the remaining men under Voigt's command fell beneath the Division Eight teams' assault. They almost had the ship.

All that means nothing though, if he kills Melissa and Tristan.

Rachel dropped down and scooted to the bow end of the bridge wing. She examined the structure of the pilothouse and came to a rapid conclusion. There was only one way to get to Voigt without going through the Vice President's daughter.

'Barry, where are you?' she said quietly in her transmitter.

※

Jason heard Rachel's question in his headset. He kept his expression neutral, his Beretta steady in his hands as he pointed the gun at Voigt.

He glanced from the mercenary to where Tristan knelt on the floor and felt fear squeeze his heart. *Not good.*

The man standing behind his best friend was starting to show signs of panic. Claire must have sensed it as well. She shifted slightly to cover the guy and the armed man next to him.

'The one who needs to put the gun down is you,' Voigt said coolly. 'I don't think your boss will be very happy if you get the Vice President's daughter killed.'

Jason stared him down. 'The U.S. government does not negotiate with terrorists.'

Voigt's expression changed. 'Let me make this simple. I'm going to ask my men to shoot your friend here in the knee.' He indicated Tristan. 'Next, I'll get them to shoot him in the gut. I hear that hurts like hell. After that, who knows where I'll ask them to—'

Rachel's voice came over the comm line. *'Get down!'*

Jason dropped to the floor with Claire and Dustin.

Light bloomed behind Voigt, an expanding, fiery cloud that mushroomed toward the sky from the ship's main deck. The bridge windows imploded, showering the ship's console and the mercenary in a hail of glittering shards. The noise and pressure waves of the blast came next, a physical presence that pushed at Jason's eardrums and nearly forced the air out of his lungs.

A figure sailed through a jagged opening behind Voigt and struck the mercenary in the back. Jason registered who it was, rolled, and shot the man behind Tristan in the chest. Tristan twisted, grabbed the gun from the dead guard's hand, and fired at the guy next to him. Claire and Dustin took out the other two men.

At the bow end of the bridge, Rachel let go of the rope she'd used to drop down from the bridge roof and tackled Voigt to the ground. Melissa shook her head dazedly on the floor a few feet away. Tristan scooted across and pulled her into his arms.

Jason's breath caught in his throat when Voigt flipped Rachel onto her back and pinned a hand to her throat. The mercenary swung his gun toward her head.

Acid flooded the back of Jason's mouth. *Too far!*

He raised his Beretta, knowing he couldn't physically get to the man in time to stop the bullet about to enter Rachel's skull. His finger froze on the trigger.

Instead of trying to break the chokehold, Rachel pushed Voigt's weapon away, locked her legs around the mercenary's neck, and rolled back.

Air left Voigt's throat in a whoosh as he was flipped up and over. He landed hard on the floor. Rachel kicked his gun out of reach, straddled his chest, and trapped his arms to his sides with her thighs.

The mercenary blinked as she grabbed his jaw, extended his neck, and pressed her Kbar against the pulsing artery in his throat.

'Just say the word, asshole,' she hissed.

In that moment, Jason decided he was going to marry Rachel Carter. He didn't know when and he didn't know how, but one thing he was sure of. He was going to make her his.

❄

CHAPTER SEVENTEEN

'I THINK I'M IN LOVE,' SAID HUCK.

It was an hour past the deadline set by the group who had kidnapped Melissa Hunt and Tristan Payne. Dawn had long since broken across the Gulf of Aden and sunlight painted the ocean waves in shades of gold.

WOLF and EAGLE were on the flight deck of the *USS Harrogate*. The warship was dwarfed by the *Bonneville*, which sat in the water next to it. Amidship, the blaze in one of the tanker's cargo bays had finally been doused. Although the effects of the explosion that had distracted Voigt in the moments preceding his capture had been pretty spectacular, Barry had made sure to set it off in a controlled manner so as not to endanger the entire vessel.

Voigt and the few men who had survived the assault were now in the custody of the U.S. Government. As for Melissa Hunt, a helicopter carrying the U.S. Vice President was on its way to the *USS Harrogate* to pick her up.

Lea followed Huck's gaze to where Jessica was checking WOLF's equipment further along the deck. 'You fall in love with anything between the ages of twenty and fifty with a pulse and two X chromosomes.'

'That woman is deadly with a gun,' said Huck, his eyes bright with heated admiration. 'And the way she wields a blade makes me want to go under the knife.'

'That's sick,' said Barry.

'Yep,' muttered Will.

'Besides, she looks like she eats guys like you for breakfast,' said Lea.

'I don't mind being eaten.'

A collective groan rose from EAGLE.

❄

'We identified the man in the Panama hat.'

Jason glanced at Rachel before focusing on the video call from Addis Ababa. Clint had just called into the *USS Harrogate*'s CIC.

'It's Senator Carrigan,' said EAGLE's XO grimly. 'FBI took him into custody an hour ago. It seems he was trying to force the Vice President's vote on a key policy for oil exploration in East Africa. The drug cartel had been buying and stealing thousands of acres of land prime for such a venture over the last eight years. Carrigan was in on it. He contacted Hunt just before four this morning and told him he would negotiate an extension of the deadline the cartel had set for executing his daughter. In exchange, Hunt would have to say yes to the oil exploration policy. The date for the vote was today.'

'What will happen to him?' said Jason.

'He's facing terrorism and extortion charges,' said Clint. 'From what Alex said, he'll be behind bars for a long time.'

Rachel and Jason took a couple more calls from Washington before calling it a day.

'We're going to have to go through a full debrief when we get back anyway,' said Jason.

'That's true,' Rachel murmured.

They walked out into the sunlight bathing the flight deck just as a helicopter appeared on the skyline. Moments later, the Sikorsky UH-60 carrying the Vice President landed on the *USS Harrogate*.

Two armed soldiers escorted Melissa Hunt to where her father stood waiting for her. Alan Hunt engulfed his daughter in his arms, his face full of elation. He let go of her when she murmured a protest, anguish replacing his joy. She smiled and took his hand.

Tristan had told Jason of Melissa Hunt's courage in the hands of her captors. By the sound of things, the young woman's tenacity had bowled him over.

The Vice President insisted on shaking the hand of every Division Eight member involved in the rescue of his daughter, much to their embarrassment. When he got to Tristan, he gave the former Ranger a hug.

Captain Taylor saw the Hunts to the helicopter as they got ready to leave. Moments before she climbed into the aircraft, Melissa Hunt crossed the flight deck, grabbed Tristan by his shoulders, and kissed him forcefully. Shock flashed across his face for a moment. Then his arms closed around her and he returned the kiss.

Catcalls echoed across the flight deck. Captain Taylor frowned. Alan Hunt stood watching his daughter with a bemused expression.

'You dog, you!' Huck yelled out to Tristan.

Jason groaned. 'Oh Christ.'

'What?' said Rachel.

She was smiling slightly as she watched the kissing couple slowly detangle themselves from each other, their faces flushed.

'I don't even want to think about the paperwork I'm going to have to fill out to explain that.'

Rachel laughed.

❄

EPILOGUE

Rachel grimaced as she eyed the meager contents of her fridge. Grocery shopping was well overdue. She picked up her phone and was dialing for pizza when her doorbell rang. She paused and frowned, finger hovering above the touchscreen.

The bell rang again. Rachel slipped the cell into the back pocket of her shorts and took her gun out of her jacket. She negotiated the boxes crowding the hallway of her apartment, looked through the peephole, and froze.

She relaxed her grip on the gun and took a deep breath to calm the sudden nervous flutter in her stomach. She opened the door. Cold air washed over her. It brought with it the smell of pepperoni and cologne.

'About time,' said Jason.

He stood on her porch, a six pack in one hand and a pizza box from her favorite Italian restaurant in the other. Rachel eyed the blue Mustang parked behind her Audi and felt his gaze skim her figure.

She shifted, conscious of her running shorts, crop top, and the lanky strands of sweat-soaked hair clinging to her temples and nape. In the face of his white shirt, denim jeans, and clean-shaven look, she felt like a hot mess.

Judging by the expression in Jason's eyes, he didn't seem to mind.

A smile curved his lips and he cocked an eyebrow. 'Do you greet all your guests with a loaded weapon?'

Rachel folded her arms and leaned against the doorjamb, the gun still in hand. 'How did you get this address? I only moved here ten days ago.'

'Zac,' said Jason with a shrug. 'Pippa helped.'

Rachel ignored the tantalizing smell of soap drifting from his tanned skin and leveled a stern stare at him. 'You know they can get into trouble for that, right?'

His smile widened. 'So, you going to invite me in?'

Rachel chewed her lip. Common sense dictated she say no. Not only did Division Eight frown on relationships between team members, having Jason Scott in her space was just too dangerous for her peace of mind.

Her stomach chose that moment to let out a loud grumble. She looked at his peace offerings, sighed, and stepped aside.

'If you touch that pizza before I get out of the shower, you're a dead man.'

Half an hour later, Rachel licked her fingers clean and leaned against the backrest of her sofa with a contented sigh. Jason sat at the other end, feet up on a stack of boxes, his second beer in hand.

'You ain't done much unpacking,' he said, looking around the bare room.

Rachel followed his gaze. 'I've been kinda busy filling out paperwork.'

He grimaced. 'You too, huh?'

She grabbed another bottle of beer. 'Comes with the territory, I guess. Alex must have it worse. From what I gather, he's been grilled by Congress about what went down on that ship.'

Jason grunted. 'Caldwell will have his back. Besides, we saved Melissa Hunt's life. I doubt the Vice President will look on quietly if they seriously mess with Division Eight. '

They sat in companionable silence for a while. Rachel finally put her beer down and looked at him steadily. The fluttering in her stomach had not abated. If anything, it had gotten worse in the last hour.

Still, she had to know. 'What are you doing here?'

Jason returned her stare, his blue eyes hooded. 'I wanted to see you.'

His voice had gone quiet, soft even.

Rachel felt her mouth go dry. 'Why?'

'Because this,' he waved at the air between them, 'whatever this is, it's not going to go away.'

Her heart started a wild drumming against her ribs.

'I know what Benjamin meant to you,' said Jason. 'I'm not trying to replace him. And I know you're probably not ready for any kind of relationship. Still, I have to know if there is a chance. For this.' He ran a hand through his hair, a hint of vulnerability flashing across his face and underscoring his words. 'For us.'

Rachel watched him for a long time, her mind filled with a myriad of emotions. *Sink or swim, Carter.*

She closed the distance between them, took his drink, and placed it on the floor. Jason stared at her, a silent question in his eyes. Rachel answered it with a kiss.

In her heart, she knew. Benjamin would have wanted this. He would have wanted her to find happiness again, even if it meant in the arms of another man. And, more than that, kissing Jason Scott felt right. In fact, it felt more than right.

By the time she took her lips off his, they were both hot and breathless.

'Are you sure about this?' Jason said above her, cheeks flushed and eyes glittering with passion.

Rachel blinked, surprised to find herself on her back, thighs wrapped shamelessly around his hips and fingers halfway down the buttons of his shirt.

Damn, he's a good kisser, she thought, dazed.

His hands moved on her skin beneath her T-shirt. She shivered at his touch, leaned up, and curled her arms around his neck.

'Bedroom's down the corridor,' she whispered in his ear.

He shuddered and lifted her in his arms. Rachel buried her face in his neck as he crossed the room. His strong pulse thrummed against her cheek, matching the beat of her own heart. She kissed the skin over it. Jason groaned, his grip tightening on her. He stormed inside the bedroom and dropped her on the bed.

They weren't subtle and they weren't gentle. As she lost herself to the hot, spine-tingling pleasure she found in Jason's arms, Rachel finally felt the chains around her heart shatter. He kissed every inch of her body, his mouth lingering on her scars and his fingers wringing hoarse cries from her throat. It felt like hours before they finally collapsed in a sweaty tangle of limbs, their heated gasps filling the moonlit room.

When her heartbeat finally slowed, Rachel rolled over, folded her arms on Jason's chest, and dropped her chin on her hands. He opened his eyes and gave her a sultry smile.

Her pulse jumped. 'How are we going to explain this to Alex?'

Jason propped himself on a pillow and pulled her up until she lay fully against him. 'I don't think you need to worry about that.'

Her skin tingled where they touched.

Desire licked at her toes once more. 'Why?'

'Let's just say it would be a case of the pot calling the kettle black if he said a word about it.'

Rachel stared at him, bemused. His meaning finally sank in.

She drew in a sharp breath. '*No way!* Alex and Vivian?'

Jason grinned. 'Uh-huh. Saw it with my own two eyes.'

Rachel's jaw dropped. 'You did *what?*'

'I walked in on them at a function in Washington. Vivian took it in her stride. Alex wouldn't look me in the eye for days.'

Her mind spun. 'Wow. Alex and Vivian, huh?'

Jason grunted. 'My source tells me they aren't the only Division Eight members in a relationship.'

Surprise flashed through Rachel. 'Who the hell is this source?'

'A drinking buddy.'

She stared at him for a moment before dropping her head on his chest.

'What are you thinking about?' he said after a while.

'WOLF and EAGLE,' she murmured. 'They're not exactly going to be thrilled if they find out we're dating.'

'We're dating?' Jason said in shocked tones.

She hit him in the ribs.

'I suspect Clint will want to punch me in the face,' said Jason.

Rachel frowned. 'Why?'

Jason's expression sobered. 'He dotes on you.'

'We're good friends,' she said quietly.

'I know.'

Rachel chewed her lip. 'You're right, though. He's gonna have words when he finds out I'm falling for you.' She let out a low groan. 'I feel a big brother talk coming on.'

Jason tucked his fingers under her chin and gazed into her eyes. 'You're falling for me?'

Rachel grimaced. 'Too soon?'

'Na-huh.'

He flipped her on her back and dropped a toe-curling kiss on her lips. Rachel's breath caught in her throat at the expression in his hot blue gaze. He lowered his mouth to her neck, lavished kisses on her skin, and started to make his way down her body.

'Too intense?' she whispered, shivering under his touch.

'No. Intense is good,' he said from somewhere around her midriff.

'Oh.'

A slow grin curved Rachel's lips. Then he did something with his mouth that made her forget all about Division Eight and their teams.

THE END

❄

The Division Eight Teams' adventures continue in Mission: Armor.

ACKNOWLEDGMENTS

To CJ Lyons, who made this new series possible. Thank you for being an inspiration and a role model.

To my friends and family. I couldn't do this without you.

Thank you for reading Mission:Black. If you enjoyed my book, please consider leaving a review on Goodreads or on the store where you purchased it. Reviews help readers like you find my books and I truly appreciate your honest opinions about my stories.

Make sure to sign up to my store newsletter for special deals on my books and new release alerts. Or you can sign up to my author newsletter to get upcoming release notifications, sneak peeks, and giveaways.

FACTS AND FICTIONS

Now, for one of my favorite parts of writing my books. Here are the facts and fictions behind the story.

Dirty Bombs

The growing global market for illicit nuclear material is a real one and has been a source of concern for the UN Security Council and its member states for a number of years. Highly enriched uranium in particular is in demand by nations seeking nuclear weapons and those wanting to maintain existing arsenals. The risk that at some point, a terrorist organization may use a dirty bomb consisting of conventional explosives and radioactive material, is very much real.

SCIF

The Sensitive Compartmented Information Facility or SCIF that EAGLE and WOLF use in Ethiopia is factual. You have undoubtedly seen these in use on TV and in movies, where they often take the shape of a glass box the characters go into to have a secure conversation. Entire buildings can be converted into SCIFs and portable ones are in regular use by the army. I thought having a SCIF inside a shiny, black shipping container on the back of a semi-trailer truck would be uber cool for the Division Eight teams.

GPS devices
Implantable GPS chips like the ones Melissa Hunt had on her body have been in use for years.

Body cameras
Body cameras are routinely used by law enforcement and federal agencies as well as the army to capture footage to direct live missions and for use as evidence in court. Although a lot of law enforcement agencies still have their officers physically load footage to a database on a daily basis, the technology to upload live to a cloud server does exist.

Voigt's Military Decoration
The Golden Leopard, South Africa's highest military decoration for bravery, is factual. Ulrich Voigt's professional background and progression to working for a private military contractor is a very common scenario for soldiers who leave the army.

GAIT Technology
The GAIT analysis software mentioned in the book

is factual. The technology has advanced in leaps and bounds in recent years and is already being used in the healthcare industry to improve diagnosis and treatment for patients. GAIT recognition technology for biometric identification and forensics is still however in its infancy, although I expect to see it in use before the end of this decade. Hopefully, it won't be as huge as the one featured in Mission Impossible 5 Rogue Nation!

Photo identifying markers

Modern smartphones and digital cameras embed GPS coordinates as well as date and time data for each photo we take, unless we disable these features or strip this metadata from the JPEG file afterward. Another reason to be careful about sharing pictures online, although many image-sharing services do automatically remove geolocation details for privacy reasons.

Ship Automatic Identification System

AIS tracking is factual and enable vessel traffic services and maritime authorities to track ships all over the world, for fishing fleet monitoring, security, and accident investigation. The data is actively used by ships for collision avoidance, navigation, and in search and rescue situations.

UAV

The MQ-9 Reaper unmanned aerial vehicle is factual and is one of the drones is use by the U.S. Army.

Camp Lemonnier is indeed the U.S. Africa Command base in Djibouti.

USS Harrogate

Although the name *USS Harrogate* is fictional, the structural and operational details of the amphibious transport dock warship are accurate.

SEAL Delivery vehicle

The Mark 8 Mod 1 manned submersible or SDV is factual and is in use by Navy SEALs. It will soon to be replaced by SWCS, Shallow Water Combat Submersible, and DCS, Dry Combat Submersible. These will be fully enclosed, as opposed to the current SDV which is open to water, and be able to carry more commandos at greater distances and depths.

DARPA Geckskin

The Geckskin gloves and boot covers mentioned in the book are factual and are part of DARPA's Z-man programs, which aim to develop biologically inspired climbing aids that can enable soldiers to scale vertical walls while carrying a full combat load, without using ropes or ladders. They were revealed to the public in 2014 and may soon be used in live missions.

Oil Exploration in East Africa

With vast untapped oil and gas resources buried deep beneath Africa and its territorial waters, the continent has become the new frontier for oil and gas exploration, with dozens of companies vying for licenses and established offshore platforms already in use. This is a source of much concern for environmental activists and international agencies worried about the ecological impact and worsening wealth inequalities such activity will engender in underdeveloped or developing countries with unstable governments and economies, rife corruption, and poor environment protection programs.

And that's it for the science and technology lesson folks!

BOOKS BY A.D. STARLING

SEVENTEEN NOVELS

Hunted

Warrior

Empire

Legacy

Origins

Destiny

SEVENTEEN SHORT STORIES

First Death

Dancing Blades

The Meeting

The Warrior Monk

The Hunger

The Bank Job

LEGION

Blood and Bones

Fire and Earth

Awakening

Forsaken

Hallowed Ground

Heir

Legion

WITCH QUEEN

The Darkest Night

Rites of Passage

Of Flames and Crows

Midnight Witch

A Fury of Shadows

Witch Queen

DIVISION EIGHT

Mission:Black

Mission: Armor

Mission:Anaconda

MISCELLANEOUS

Void - A Sci-fi Horror Short Story

The Other Side of the Wall - A Horror Short Story

ABOUT A.D. STARRLING

Visit AD Starrling's store at shop.adstarrling.com and buy her ebooks, paperbacks, hardbacks, special edition print books, and audiobooks direct

Want to know about AD Starrling's upcoming releases? Sign up to her author newsletter for new release alerts, sneak peeks, giveaways, and more

Follow AD Starrling on Amazon

Join AD's reader group on Facebook
The Seventeen Club

Check out this link to find out more about A.D. Starrling
Linktr.ee/AD_Starrling

Printed in Great Britain
by Amazon